MW01041283

Also by Monica Hughes

Gold-Fever Trail
Crisis on Conshelf Ten
Earthdark
The Tomorrow City
The Ghost Dance Caper
Beyond the Dark River
The Keeper of the Isis Light
The Guardian of Isis
The Isis Pedlar
Hunter in the Dark
Ring-Rise, Ring-Set
The Beckoning Lights
The Treasure of the Long Sault
Space Trap
My Name is Paula Popowich!
Devil on my Back
Sandwriter
The Dream Catcher
Blaine's Way
Log Jam
The Promise
The Refuge
Little Fingerling (Ill. Brenda Clark)
Invitation to the Game
The Crystal Drop
A Handful of Seeds (Ill. Luis Garay)
The Golden Aquarians
Castle Tourmandyne
Where Have You Been, Billy Boy?
The Seven Magpies
The Faces of Fear
The Story Box
The Other Place

stormWARNING

stormWARNING

monica
HUGHES

HarperCollins*Publishers*Ltd

STORM WARNING
Copyright © 2000 by Monica Hughes.
All rights reserved. No part of this book
may be used or reproduced in any
manner whatsoever without prior written permission except in the case of brief
quotations embodied in reviews.
For information address
HarperCollins Publishers Ltd.,
55 Avenue Road, Suite 2900,
Toronto, Ontario, Canada M5R 3L2.

www.harpercanada.com

HarperCollins books may be purchased
for educational, business, or sales
promotional use. For information please
write: Special Markets Department,
HarperCollins Canada,
55 Avenue Road, Suite 2900,
Toronto, Ontario, Canada M5R 3L2.

First edition

Canadian
Cataloguing in Publication Data

Hughes, Monica, 1925–
Storm warning

I S B N 0-00-648550-2

I. Title.

PS8565.U34S76 2000
jC813'.54   C00-931206-4
PZ7.H84St 2000

00 01 02 03 04 HC 6 5 4 3 2 1

Printed and bound in the United States
Set in New Aster

Thanks to Priscilla Galloway for checking my scuba diving and sailing facts.

StormWARNING

chapter ONE

I COULD FEEL him staring at me—a prickly sensation at the back of my neck. I turned casually and looked around, my hand shading my eyes, so he wouldn't notice I was checking on him. Small boats were bobbing at their moorings in the harbour; kids were running up and down the dock, leaning over the edge, pointing out fish in the crystal clear water. I looked at the people behind me in the lineup, all waiting for the boat to take us out to the dive site.

He was there, behind a couple in their twenties. Not a face to forget. Short curly blond hair and a great tan. The usual uniform of T-shirt and shorts. Piercing blue eyes in a distinctive bony face, like the face of one of those aristocrats on British TV.

We'd been on one dive together already—I'd made sure of that—exploring the two wrecks close under the surface near the harbour. And we'd had lunch in the same coffee shop close to the dock, but at separate tables. I thought he was going to make a move then, but he didn't. Later, when I'd strolled along the street looking for postcards to send to high school friends back home, I'd seen him in the reflection of a store window. Looking across at me.

I was playing it so cool as I waited in line for the boat, but inside I was a mess of emotions. I was on the brink of success—the plan that Dad and Mom and I had talked over for the past year was actually working. There was a wicked edge of excitement in pretending to be what I was not. But I felt something else I wasn't expecting—an attraction to this guy that had my heart thumping. I could feel myself flush as he looked at me, and I forced myself to turn away, to concentrate on what I *had* to do.

The dive boat nosed up to the dock and we began to board. "You on your own? Need a diving buddy?" Chuck, the dive master, asked me. I'd already talked to him after the morning's dive, saying I was alone and kind of interested in the cute blond guy. He had laughed and was ready to play Cupid.

"If you can set me up with someone, that'd be great." I spoke clearly so my voice would carry over the chatter around me.

"This afternoon we'll be diving at sixty feet. You comfortable with that?"

I smiled at him. "Theoretically, anyway," I said lightly.

"Then I'll make sure you're paired with an experienced diver. Hey, here's just the guy! You'll be fine with him. Bry, how are you doing?"

"Great, thanks, Chuck. What can I do for you?"

"Partner this young lady on the dive. This is Bryan MacDonald, a local. His family lives on the north shore. Miss . . . ?"

"Sandra Williams. I'm on holiday with my family. Hi."

We sat down next to each other as the driver revved the engine and headed out.

"So what are you doing back here, Bry? You must have explored these wrecks a dozen times," Chuck said.

Good question, I said to myself, and saw Bryan hesitate and then shrug. "Oh, one more time won't hurt."

Yes, I thought. *I know you've been hunting for a diving buddy. Now I think you're hooked.*

He saw me looking at him and I turned away casually so he wouldn't see the triumph in my eyes. Instead, I glanced over the shadow side of the launch into water that was as clear as glass all the way down to the limestone bottom. An enticing blue-green world beckoned me. It was a perfect day, and I would have revelled in it if I hadn't had other things on my mind.

The dive boat chugged slowly past the inshore wrecks and made its way to the dive site, avoiding other boats and the many buoys flying the distinctive red flags with the white diagonal stripe that warned of divers below. The engine stopped, and the boat was tied up to a permanent mooring at the site.

As we pulled on our wetsuits, Chuck began telling us the history of this particular wreck, sunk on the limestone reef in 1879. It had slid off the ridge of the reef and settled in sixty feet of water. "You've got about forty-five minutes to explore the area," he concluded. "But remember, that time depends on how much energy you expend. I want you all back at the boat with five hundred pounds in your tanks. Okay? Any questions?"

"Can we go inside this wreck?" someone inquired.

I felt a shiver down my spine. This was my own personal nightmare—being trapped inside a wreck with my air running out. *Come on, Sandra,* I told myself bracingly. *You'd better get used to the idea. If all goes well, you'll have to face that hazard some day soon.*

But not today, thankfully. "It's open to the water on one side," Chuck was saying. "It's okay to explore that part, although you'll have to watch out for snags. But

3

don't attempt to go through into the rest of the ship. That's for experts only. This is just a recreational dive. Everyone understand?"

Bryan turned to help me with my buoyancy compensator vest and tank. I snugged the straps and put on my weight belt before helping him with his equipment. Then we checked each other out, saying the steps aloud, and finally waited our turn on the platform at the stern of the boat to pull on fins over our boots.

"Ready?"

I nodded and stepped out, hand to mask. When I surfaced, I cleared my snorkel and looked around at the other divers bobbing on the water. Then, at a signal from Chuck, I exchanged snorkel for regulator, vented my buoyancy vest and sank slowly beneath the surface.

The sun-dazzle gave way to clear blue-green light; it was like being inside an emerald. I descended slowly, pulling myself down the anchor rope, watching the colours slowly darken and grey. As the pressure of the water increased I cleared my ears and got rid of the squeeze in my mask almost automatically. When I saw Bryan stop, I adjusted my buoyancy and hovered beside him, with my fins just clearing the bottom. Though I knew this lake was primarily limestone, there was enough of a residue of fine sand and mud to stir up the bottom and spoil our view if we kicked it with our fins.

Directly above us the anchor line disappeared towards the surface. To our right was the shadowy hulk we'd come to explore. Coated with greyish silt, the wooden wreck lay on its side. I kicked slowly along, my fingers lightly touching the gaping hole in the hull

4

where the unforgiving knife-edge of the limestone ridge had ripped through so many years ago.

I found myself imagining the crew and passengers. The women would have been encumbered with heavy woollen skirts, layers of petticoats and tight corsets. Even if they knew how to swim—which was doubtful in those days—they wouldn't have stood a chance. I imagined myself struggling helplessly in the storm waters . . . Even if there had been lifeboats, or loose planks for the survivors to cling to, the water would have been icy. Despite my wetsuit, I was conscious of the coldness of this northern lake.

I shivered, imagining the bones of the drowned strewn on the lake bottom. *Stupid*, I told myself. This was a cleared and sanitized recreational site, no longer the memorial of personal tragedy. But still I felt haunted. Perhaps it was the presence of another disaster, one much closer to home, that was casting its shadow over me.

I forced these morbid thoughts out of my head, kicked gently and rose up over the ragged edge of the hole in the hull. I looked around the deck and peered into the interior, my flashlight illuminating small details one by one. Below me, my light caught an unusual shape. Face down, parallel to the sloping deck, I peered into the darkness and distinguished the outline of a bell—the ship's bell. Dislodged from its position by the steering wheel, it now lay on its side, half-filled with sand. Mute, no longer measuring out the half-hours of a working ship's day and night watches.

A wave of sadness washed over me at the thought of all those lives so suddenly cut off, and I told myself not to be silly: every one of the people aboard this wreck would be dead now anyway, over a hundred years later. *But dying at the end of one's natural span isn't the same thing as dying unexpectedly, without warning.*

I backed slowly away and turned to look for Bryan. My heart jumped, for he had been swimming just behind me. In my solitary underwater world, where the only sounds were my breathing and the slow escape of bubbles from my regulator, I had not heard him. For the moment we were alone, looking at each other, with no one else in sight.

I had turned away again, ready to go on with my exploration, when he reached out and almost casually flipped my face mask off. It happened so fast I didn't have time to think. Cold water slapped my face. I could no longer see clearly, just the smear of water against my eyes. For a split second I could feel myself panicking, wanting to scream, to flounder up to the surface, to do all the things that were wrong and dangerous.

The panic lasted only a second and then training took over, the routine that had been drilled into me at the pool back home where I had first learned to scuba dive. *Stop. Breathe deeply. Think. Breathe deeply.*

I reached up with both hands, groped for my mask and pulled it gently but firmly down over my face again. I took several deep breaths through the regulator in my mouth, then looked up, tilting my head back, pressing the top of the mask against my forehead. As I exhaled slowly through my nose, I could feel the icy water slowly draining from the bottom of my mask. It worked, just as it had worked in the pool back home.

Once the mask was clear and I could see again, I no longer felt helpless. I turned to face him, furiously angry, wanting to strike out at my so-called buddy. I drew my hand across my neck in an explicit throat-cutting gesture and shook my fist at him. He raised his hands in surrender. He couldn't smile, of course, with the regulator distorting his mouth, but I could swear that, behind the mask, his blue eyes were laughing at me.

Laughing? Is he on to me? Surely he can't guess why I'm really here. The thought flashed through my mind and I felt suddenly vulnerable. Knowing that I was breathing too deeply, and feeling angrier than ever, I signalled that I was going up. A little over five hundred psi still remained in my tank, but the mood of the afternoon was ruined, and beneath my anger I was also a bit afraid. I swam towards where the rope snaked up towards the light and began my ascent, slowly venting my buoyancy control vest as I rose.

It was tempting to rip up to the surface, to pull off my regulator and scream at Bryan MacDonald—and at Chuck for saddling me with this dangerous young man. *Go up slowly,* I had to remind myself. *No faster than the bubbles from my regulator.*

The bubbles slowly drifting up past my face had their usual calming effect. *It was your choice, Sandra,* I reminded myself. *You picked this guy. You asked the dive master to introduce you. Now you're stuck with him, for better or worse. Or you could back away from the whole enterprise . . . which isn't an option,* I told myself grimly, *not now that I've come this close.*

But why had he done such a reckless thing as to tear off my mask? Was he just showing me he was in charge? Maybe he suspected what I was after. But he couldn't possibly know that, could he? I'd covered my tracks too well.

Am I the bait—or is he? I thought, resting at the

fifteen-foot level, my hand on the anchor rope, watching the numbers on my watch click slowly over. Bryan was hovering just below me. If he tried anything stupid now, I could kick free and hit the surface.

Time. I came up into daylight and dancing water. Into the real world. Had that weird incident really happened? Automatically I reinflated my buoyancy control vest and swam to the steps of the dive boat.

Sitting on the steps, I took off my weight belt and fins, and handed them up to the skipper before climbing on board myself. "The guy that Chuck landed me with—he deliberately pulled off my mask. I thought Chuck said he was to be trusted!"

"Bry?" The man's astonishment was so obvious that again I wondered if I'd dreamed the whole event.

Behind my shoulder Bryan laughed.

I whipped around and glared up into his dancing blue eyes. "It's not funny."

"Sorry." He didn't look in the least contrite. "I was just testing—I needed to know your reaction. Seriously. Hey, give me a chance to explain."

"There's really nothing to explain." I turned away coldly, and let the skipper help me off with my tank and buoyancy vest. Two by two the other divers surfaced and began to remove their equipment, with Chuck shepherding the stragglers aboard. In the happy chatter the icy silence between Bryan and me went unnoticed. I peeled off my wetsuit, towelled off and put on my T-shirt and shorts over my swimsuit, then packed my gear back in its bag.

Back at the wharf Chuck caught my arm. "Miss Williams, I just heard your complaint. Honestly, I'm dumbfounded. I've never known Bry MacDonald to do

anything reckless, engage in horseplay or anything that
might endanger his partner on a dive. It's beyond me."

"Me too." I managed a smile. "He scared me and
made me furious, spoiled my afternoon—but I guess
that's all. It's my fault. I asked you to partner us."

"There *must* be some logical explanation."

"That's what he said—but logical? I doubt it."

"Maybe you should listen to him."

"Maybe." I picked up my equipment bag and went
ashore. "Or maybe not." I walked down the wharf,
angry, not at the incident now, but because my carefully
laid plans seemed to be ruined. Whether he suspected
me or not, the scheme had all gone wrong. I felt as if I'd
been angling for a trout and had caught a shark instead.

I was suddenly conscious of him waiting at the end of
the wharf. I couldn't smile or apologize. He was the
guilty party. I walked past him as if he were invisible,
even though I knew he'd never talk to me again if I
ignored him—knew that I shouldn't let my anger spoil
all my plans. But he surprised me by reaching out and
taking the equipment bag from my hand.

"Hey! What do you think you're doing?"

"Carry your bag, lady? You're staying at the hotel,
aren't you?"

"It's only a block away. I can certainly carry my own
equipment, thank you," I snapped.

"No problem." He smiled, a smile that at any other
time would have won me over totally. But not right now.

"You'd like to shower and change, I expect," he went
on, apparently impervious to my anger. "Clean off your
equipment and suit. Would a couple of hours be
enough? Then I'll pick you up for dinner. Say six
o'clock?"

"You're taking a lot for granted," I said angrily. "Suppose I've got other plans?"

"But I thought you didn't know anyone here. You said you were vacationing."

"I'm here with my parents, if it's any of your business."

"I'm sure they'll spare you for one evening. Will they be at the hotel waiting for you?"

"I don't know. Maybe. But that's not the point . . ."

"Here's your bag. Six o'clock in the foyer."

"Oh, really, you're too much!"

"Then I *will* explain. And apologize properly. I know a place that has great seafood."

I found myself standing at the hotel's entrance, bag in hand, my mouth open to make some brilliant retort— but I didn't have time to deliver it before he was gone. I pushed the door open and went to the desk for my key. Only when I had calmed down did I realize that my plan to snare him seemed to have worked after all.

"So he's asked me out to dinner." I sat on the edge of Dad and Mom's bed, swinging my legs.

"You sound a bit doubtful. Sandra, do you really want to go ahead with this?"

I stared at my father, at the frown creasing his forehead. "But you helped Mom and me plan this from the very beginning. I can't back out now."

"I know I did. But suddenly the idea of your going out with this particular young man doesn't seem so smart."

I threw my arm over his shoulder and kissed his cheek. "I *am* sixteen, Dad. And totally in control." Then I suddenly remembered the frightening instant when Bryan had flipped off my mask. I smiled confidently.

No, I won't tell them about that little incident. It would only worry them.

As if reading my thoughts, Mom echoed my words. "Totally in control? Oh, love, take care. Don't be reckless. I know you want to go through with this for my sake. I'm the one who needs answers. But not if getting them puts you at risk."

"Come on, you two. You're so solemn all of a sudden. It's only dinner. Getting to know him. Nothing to worry about. Maybe nothing'll come of it. Or maybe he'll bite. But either way, I'll have an evening out."

I psyched myself up to believe what I'd just told them. After my shower I brushed my hair till it shone and put on a flattering new top over my jeans. The mirror in my hotel room told me I looked okay, and the appreciation in Bryan's eyes confirmed it. I put the future out of my head for the minute and told myself firmly that I was going to have a good time.

The restaurant was busy but not too noisy, and the seafood was great, as Bryan had promised. He was easy to talk to, and listened as if he really cared. "I aim to be a marine biologist, working in the field," I told him. "Imagine being able to dive and getting paid for it! And maybe I'll be able to find out more about why the marine world is changing: fish stocks moving, vanishing. I'd like to have a hand in replenishing them." It was a good cover story and I was proud of it. I had worked it out with Dad and Mom the previous winter, when we were planning this adventure.

"You sound like an idealist."

"Maybe I am. Or maybe I'd just like to go on eating great meals like this." I made a joke of it, not wanting to get too serious, afraid of getting carried away and saying more than I meant to. "What about you, Bryan? Do you have a burning ambition?"

"Only a short-term one. When that's behind me, maybe I'll be able to concentrate on the big picture."

"Like getting through high school?" I said, smiling.

"That too."

The waiter cleared away our plates and we ordered dessert and coffee. The interruption caused an uneasy silence. We broke it together.

"Bryan, I need to know . . ."

"Sandra, I promised I'd explain . . ."

We looked at each other and laughed. "Okay, Bryan," I said, "go ahead and explain. I can't wait."

"About the mask. I did have a sensible reason."

"*Sensible*? Suppose I'd panicked?"

"That was it. That's what I needed to find out. How good a diver you really were."

I felt my heart flip. This was it. *Go slowly*, I warned myself. "Why would it matter to you?" I asked cautiously. "We met on a dive, that's all. Hello. Goodbye."

"Maybe not goodbye. Not yet anyway. How long are you staying?"

This was it then. I took a deep, steadying breath and let it out with a deliberately dramatic sigh. "Only another couple of days at most. It's such a pain. Mom and Dad are exploring northern Ontario, attending auctions, picking up stuff for their shop. They're into antiques, you see."

"Interesting—I guess," he said in a flat voice.

Encouraged, I burst out, "I just hate auctions. All that standing around. I'd much rather stay here and go on diving."

"Why can't you?"

"Mom and Dad would never let me stay here on my own. Not while I'm still only sixteen. They're kind of old-fashioned."

"You could stay with me," he said abruptly, and I drew back, deliberately misunderstanding.

"*What?*"

"I mean with me and my mom and dad and grandmother and kid sister."

I laughed. "You had me worried for a second. I thought I'd read you wrong. Well, that's a great offer, Bryan, but what would your parents think about your inviting home a stranger—just like that? Not to mention your grandmother and kid sister."

"Oh, Amanda'd be thrilled. The others too. You'd like it. We live across the bay, on the north shore." He gestured vaguely out of the restaurant window at the expanse of lake. "We've got a good dock and a launch and a runabout. Our own tanks. We could dive there or come back and do some more exploring here. What do you say?"

I drew a somewhat shaky breath. "It sounds like a dream come true. But . . ."

"But what?"

"What you did—flipping off my mask. To tell you the truth, it still bothers me. Why was it important to know how I'd behave in an emergency? What sort of emergency did you have in mind? And I can't help asking myself, what do I know about you? Not a whole lot."

"I promise I'll explain everything. About me. About . . . oh, a whole lot of things. But first I need you to say you'll come."

Deliberately I hesitated. *It's like fishing*, I thought. *You*

13

snag the fish, but if the hook isn't deep enough, it'll shake its head and be off. You have to be patient—wait for the right second. Then reel it in. That's the question: is now the right time? Then I found myself thinking again about the trout and the shark. Which was Bryan? Trout? Or shark?

"Come on." His voice was very persuasive. "I know you're sold on the idea. How long can you stay? Two weeks? Three?"

"Hold on." I laughed. "Ten days max. And only if I can square it with my parents."

"Let's go and ask them now." He signalled the waiter for the bill.

"Not tonight. I need to talk to them first. Soften them up. Could we meet for breakfast tomorrow?"

"Sure. Eight o'clock okay?"

"Hey, we're on holiday. Better make it eight-thirty. In the hotel coffee shop. And I'll need . . ." I hesitated.

"To know more about me. Sure. Your parents can ask around. My family's well known here. And of course they can phone and talk to Mom or Dad."

"And what about me? I don't know you at all, Bryan MacDonald."

"A week or so will change that. Though I suppose you might find me really boring. My life's an open book," he said lightly.

An open book? I suddenly remembered the secret diary I'd kept in junior high, its key always round my neck. *How deep are you in?* I wondered. *How much do you really know?*

I smiled and nodded. "All right. I'll ask Dad to phone your parents and ask around in the morning. Thanks for dinner." *So far so good.*

"I'll see you back to the hotel."

"You don't have to do that."

"No problem. It's on the way to the dock."

I must have looked surprised, for he laughed. "I live on the launch when I come over here. A lot cheaper than a hotel. And more convenient. Come on."

"How'd it go?" Dad asked as soon as I stepped inside their door.

"Great seafood." I sprawled across the bed.

"You know that's not what I meant."

I managed a nervous laugh. "Right now I'm supposed to be begging you to let me join Bryan MacDonald *and* his family for ten days on the family estate. How about it, Dad? It does sound grand. A dock and *two* boats."

"That's no surprise," Mom put in sadly. "Money *and* power. We've known that since the beginning. When I was just a kid—"

"Which is why we've got to do it my way," I burst out. "You're not having second thoughts, are you, Mom?"

"Not unless *you* are. You sound jumpy, Sandra. Are you sure you want to go through with this?"

I rubbed my hands over my face and sighed, feeling really frustrated. We'd had this conversation before, more than once; sometimes Dad backed off from the plan, sometimes Mom. But whenever they did, I just got more determined. It was as if I'd caught Mom's obsession. "Yes, Mom, I'm sure. I'm just a bit tired, that's all. He'll be here for breakfast, by the way. I told him eight-thirty, not wanting to seem too eager. He's happy to have you ask around, phone his parents and so on—"

"Which we'll certainly do," Dad interrupted, "though

15

I don't expect we'll be any closer to knowing whether the young man's in the clear."

"I hope he is, Dad. I really do. He seems like a neat guy." *Except for tearing off my mask*, I thought. Again, I decided not to worry them with that incident.

"Better go and pack whatever you'll need for ten days of living with the rich and famous." Mom's voice was suddenly bitter and I flashed a quick look at her.

"Mom, I know I said they had a dock and two boats, but is it that big a deal?"

"According to the newspaper reports it's a famous architect's idea of a summer place. Remember the photographs?"

"Oh, they always exaggerate, don't they?"

"I wouldn't count on it. You'll need to pack a couple of nice dresses as well as your swimsuits." Mom hesitated, and I saw her bite her lip. "Sandra, are you *sure* you want to go through with this?"

"Absolutely. Mom, don't worry. And, Dad, take that frown off your face. Goodnight."

"See you in the morning, love. Sleep well."

Sleep well, indeed! I lay and stared at the ceiling, sleep light-years away. Then I sat up and punched my pillow. *Stupid*, I scolded myself. *There's nothing to be gained by lying here worrying. I can't plan ahead. All I can do is play it by ear and snatch the opportunity if it's offered. If it doesn't work out, I'll have had a holiday with the rich and famous, that's all.*

I found myself wondering just why finding the truth had become such an obsession with me. At first it had only been Mom's. But once I'd found the collection of old newspaper clippings, I'd got drawn in. Then Dad had got into the act and the discussion had sort of snow-balled, one small idea leading to another, until finally the whole grand plan had emerged. I'd taken up scuba diving and got myself certified. Diving was great and I loved it, and the idea of being a kind of private eye was exciting—in theory. But suddenly the plan was coming together in an unexpected reality. Was I ready for it? Could I handle it? I just wasn't sure. I thumped my pillow again and closed my eyes, determined to sleep.

When Bryan came striding into the coffee shop the next morning, I could see that he, at any rate, hadn't lain awake worrying. After I introduced him to Mom and Dad, he shook hands, sat down and immediately caught the waitress's eye. "Pancakes, a double order please. Bacon, sausages. Orange juice. Thanks."

Impressive, I thought. *Used to getting his own way.* "Loading up like that, you must not be planning a morning dive," I teased.

"Absolutely not. If your parents are willing to let you go, I'd like to start out right away. How about it, Mrs. Williams? Mr. Williams?"

"I've already asked around," Dad said slowly. "Your family certainly has a sterling reputation in this neigh-bourhood, Bryan. But I would still like to talk to your father or mother."

"Of course, Mr. Williams." Bryan nodded. "The phone booths are right over there, across the lobby. I'll phone them for you—the number's unlisted." He made as if to stand up, but Dad waved him down.

"No hurry. Have your breakfast first."

It arrived quickly, and Mom ordered more coffee. "Go ahead. Eat up. We'll leave you in peace," she said.

17

"Mom, you never have more than one cup of coffee," I said thoughtlessly.

She gave me a look. "Maybe I'm nervous at the thought of letting my wild daughter out of my sight."

"Mom!" What could I say, with Bryan sitting right there? Mom smiled and we looked at each other for a minute, so much unspoken between us. I remembered so clearly the day I was helping to clean up when we were moving house—the day I found the big file of clippings, the unfinished story. Then, slowly, the plan evolving. *For you, Mom*, I thought. *The truth at last.*

"Hey, you two, lighten up. It's only a ten-day holiday away from your long-suffering parents, Sandra," Dad broke in.

I forced a laugh. "Sorry, Dad. Actually I'm dying to get away. No more auctions! Yay!"

Bryan pushed his chair back. "All finished. I believe I'll last till lunch. Coming, Mr. Williams?"

Dad turned to Mom. "Would you like to talk to the MacDonalds too, Rosemary?"

Mom shook her head. "No thanks, Mike. I'll just relax over my wicked cup of coffee."

We watched Dad and Bryan cross the restaurant. "Of course, he's impossibly good-looking," Mom said casually. "You'll be careful, won't you, my dear?"

"Oh, come on, Mom! You know why I'm getting into this. Strictly business."

"I didn't mean . . . We don't know how much he's involved. I don't want you getting hurt, that's all."

I squeezed Mom's hand. "I know what you mean. Don't worry. I'll stay cool."

"I'm sure you will." Mom took a slip of paper from her purse. "Here are our phone numbers over the next ten days. Call any time if you need us. We'll never be far away. Phone us in any case. It won't look suspicious. They'll expect you to keep in touch."

We sat in silence, watching people move in and out of the coffee shop. "There they are," I said at last. It had seemed like a very long wait.

"And judging from your father's expression, it's good news."

"Well, we didn't really expect anything else, did we? Not with everything we already know," I said under my breath. "So, do I get to go, Dad?" I added out loud.

"Mrs. MacDonald was most welcoming. I think you'll have a wonderful time."

"Thank you, Dad." I got to my feet and hugged him. "I'll be off then. Just have to get my stuff from my room. 'Bye, Mom." I gave her a quick kiss. "I'll meet you in the foyer, Bryan. Five minutes."

Upstairs I took a moment to brush my teeth and reapply lipstick. Everything I needed was packed. Mom would tidy up the rest of my stuff. I looked around, took a deep breath and went downstairs with my case and equipment bag to where Bryan was waiting. I told myself that the fluttery feeling in my stomach was just nerves and had nothing to do with the good-looking suntanned young man waiting for me.

Now it begins, I told myself. *The long wait is over and the adventure begins.*

chapter TWO

IT WAS a pretty little launch, shining with blue and white paint, its name, *Moonlight*, painted on the prow. We went aboard and Bryan stowed our gear down in the cabin. I had a quick look below, at the couches built along each side, at the table with its raised rim, at the neat little galley with everything in its proper place.

"Anything I can do to help? Not that I know much about boats," I said as he came on deck again.

"Not a thing. She's a lovely motor launch. It's not like sailing. Though Grandfather used to sail alone on . . ." He stopped and fiddled with the engine. It roared into life.

"On?"

"*Far Skimmer*. A sloop Grandfather had, years and years ago."

"Pretty name." I sat down behind him, a smile pasted on my face, my heart pounding. I was thankful Bryan was busy, not looking at me. *Far Skimmer*. A name from the past. Thirty years in the past. A name I knew so well from yellowing newspaper clippings.

Bryan tamed the engine's roar to a gentle purr. Expertly he cast off the mooring lines and guided us out into the open channel. He kept well away from the dive sites and turned northeast towards the distant shore.

"There's nothing in our way now," he said after a while. "So why don't you take the wheel while I rustle up some hot chocolate?"

"Can I really?"

20

"Sure. Just keep her on this heading."

"What if another craft materializes out of thin air?"

"Then scream."

Nervously I took Bryan's place at the tiller, scanning the expanse of lake ahead of us. Since it was blue and empty and seemed totally safe, I relaxed, glancing now and then at the compass heading. The sun dazzled brightly on the water, and I fished my shades out of my pocket and put them on. A jet passed high overhead, its white contrail bisecting the sky. It was easy to imagine that the launch was mine, that I lived in a gorgeous summer home on the north shore. Rich and famous.

It can't be real, I thought. *If I pinch myself, I'll probably wake up. But I don't want to. After all the dreaming, the planning—I'm finally on my way.* I could feel my heart pounding.

Bryan climbed up the steps from the cabin with a steaming mug of chocolate in each hand. He handed me one, put his on the ledge beside him and took over the steering.

I cradled my drink in my hands. Though the sun was brilliant, the wind was surprisingly cool out on the water. "When will we get there?" I asked eagerly.

"What's your hurry? Enjoy the moment."

"I am," I protested. "Just curious, that's all. I don't even know how far away your—your summer place is."

"About forty nautical miles. It takes almost three hours because we have to slow down once we get close to shore. Lots of little islands, some no more than rocks. It's tricky. But the house is more than our summer place now. For the last few years, ever since Grandfather died, in fact, we've lived there year-round."

21

"What about school?"

"Amanda and I go to boarding schools in Toronto."

"Me too. What's yours like?"

We finished our chocolate, exchanging horror stories about school food and the awful amount of homework we had to get through. The time flew by. Finally my curiosity got the better of me. "Other than school, what's your past history?"

He shrugged. "There's not a lot to tell. School in Toronto most of the year, and here for all the important months. Grade eleven this fall."

Not much of an answer. "And then?"

"Good question. Dad would like me to follow in his footsteps, but I'm not so keen. He's a stockbroker. But the business of making money for its own sake seems kind of boring to me. I'd rather do something that makes a difference in the world. Anyway, that's all on hold for the moment. My immediate plans are on my mind the most right now."

"Hmm?" *Is he going to tell me?*

"Tell you later," he said absently, his eyes on the approaching shore.

The rocks and islets came closer, dotting the lake like pebbles thrown carelessly into a pond. Our boat slipped past islands with inaccessible rocky shores, others with tiny harbours scooped out of the greyish rock. Here I saw jetties, yachts moored and cottages clustered around. *It would be great to be an artist in this place*, I thought idly, *daubing canvases with great gobs of paint, capturing the rugged quality and the myriad colours of the lichen-patched rocks*. Once again I found myself imagining what it would be like to live here in luxury, and I forced myself away from the daydream. *You're an*

outsider, Sandra Williams, and don't you ever forget it, I
told myself sternly.

The tune of the engine changed again. We were slow-
ing down noticeably. Bryan was no longer watching the
compass but seemed to be reading the bewildering
array of buoys, easing the launch now to right, now to
left.

"How does it work? How on earth do you know what
you're doing?"

He laughed. "I've done it so many times, it's like
driving home from the local supermarket. But if I were
a stranger in town, then I'd have to read street signs,
remember how many blocks to go before turning right
and so on."

"And those buoys are like street signs?"

"That's just what they are. The red ones you leave to
your right, approaching harbour. The green ones to
your left. Only two things to worry about: too much
wind, or a fog and no wind."

"I guess some of the wrecks we explored went down
in fog."

"More likely they didn't have such accurate charts
back then. The escarpment runs right under the lake
here—a limestone reef like a knife-edge ready and waiting to cut a ship in two."

I shivered suddenly. *Someone walking over my grave.*
That's what Grandma always said. I rubbed my arms
and looked down into the dark water. Deep. No underwater rock was lurking here to slice through this pretty
launch. I knew I could trust Bryan to navigate us safely;
he must have done it hundreds of times. And he *had*
insisted that we both wear life jackets.

The sound of the engine changed again. Now we were

sliding slowly through a narrow waterway between two rocky peninsulas. Ahead were a dock and a sturdy boathouse. Wooden steps going up, up.

I caught my breath as my eyes followed the curve of the stairway to a house that hung suspended, as if it were floating, above the forested slope. Nothing like the newspaper photographs, it was huge. Not like my memories of the summer cottages I'd visited either, with their dark, cobwebby rafters, their smoking chimneys and dampness, the trudge to the outside biffy. This was a house out of *Famous Homes*.

"Here we are." Bryan's voice broke into my thoughts. "This is Treetops."

I told myself firmly that I wasn't going to be overawed by this place and the money that obviously lay behind it. *Money and power*, Mom had said, that had sheltered them from the questions that should have been asked, from the truth that had never been revealed. It was the MacDonalds' wealth and influence that had made me angry, made me bulldoze Mom and Dad into accepting the plan. The need for *justice*.

I watched Bryan's face as he approached the land. His eyes narrowed against the light flickering through the trees to our right. *Money and power*. Was he part of all that? He cut the engine and we glided slowly towards the dock. In the sudden silence I could hear a bird singing its heart out above me, way up among the treetops. *Don't be taken in*, I warned myself again. *Not by the place. Nor by them.*

"Bry, you're back!" A small figure came hurtling down the wooden steps to the dock, the sun sparkling on curly hair, hair like Bryan's, its blond colour tinged with copper red. I found I was holding my breath: surely she

24

would trip and fall any second now, she was going so fast. But the newcomer landed safely on the dock and grinned at us.

"You're back," she repeated. "About time!"

"Hey, sprout, make yourself useful." Bryan moved to the bow and tossed a line ashore. I watched as she caught it deftly and looped it twice around a bollard, then as quickly moved aft to catch the second line and haul it tight, the muscles in her small arms bunched in the effort. The launch glided quietly up to the dock.

It was obvious that the two of them had done this a hundred times before, that they were in a world where they were the masters. I felt totally small and insignificant. *Ridiculous*, I scolded myself. Bryan was just a spoiled and wealthy teenager, and the girl was only a kid, not a day over ten—maybe eleven at the most.

Then he took the wind out of my sails by holding out his hand and saying "Welcome" with a wonderful smile as he helped me ashore. "This is my kid sister, Amanda. Amanda, this is Sandra Williams."

"Hi. So you're Bry's new diving buddy. That's great. Well, I guess it is. Though it's really mean of him not to take me. I'll be twelve in October and I can dive as well as he can—pretty nearly. But I can't begin to get certified till I'm twelve, which is grossly unfair. After all—"

"Enough, Amanda. Tell me, how is everyone?"

"Oh." A shadow of a frown crossed the freckled face and was gone. "Just fine, I guess. The same as usual. You know."

I saw Bryan look intently at his sister. It was as if a silent message had passed between them. Then he gave himself a little shake. "So what are we waiting for? Let's get the show on the road." He slung my bag onto the dock.

"What about our gear?" I asked.

"We'll leave it in the boathouse. Amanda'll look after it, won't you, half-pint?" he said casually over his shoulder and set off up the stairs. "Come on, Sandra."

I hesitated, cardigan in one hand, purse in the other, noticing the disappointment on his sister's expressive face. It was so obvious that Bryan was special to her. Was I going to be in the way? "Maybe I can help you, Amanda," I suggested.

"That'd be great. D'you want to bring your dive bag ashore? I'll see to Bry's."

In the cool darkness of the boathouse I helped Amanda hang up the suits on a sturdy railing along one wall, where a small-sized suit already hung. "Gathering dust, you'll notice." Amanda sighed dramatically. "I hardly *ever* get to scuba dive now. Last year Bry spent ages teaching me. This year everything's changed. He's got this bug."

"Bug?"

"Yeah. Something he plans to do. It's a deep secret he won't talk about. But don't worry. He'll have to tell *you*, of course," she added darkly.

"Will he?" I asked lightly, though my heart thumped. She didn't answer and I went on. "Do you spend all summer here?"

"You bet. It's heaven. The best place in the world. I wish we could stay all year. But there's school and all that stuff. What a waste."

"Cheer up. School does get interesting. And you can always plan an underwater career. That's what I'm going to do—be a marine biologist." I decided to try out my imaginary career on Bryan's sister.

"Wow." Amanda's eyes widened. "Tell me every single thing about it. Will I have to be good at math? I'm not great at it right now, but I'll work on it if it's important."

"Aren't you a bit young to make up your mind about your future?"

Amanda frowned. "I really am almost twelve," she protested. "I'm just scrawny. Mom says I'm bound to fill out and I mustn't be impatient. But I think—Darn, there's the lunch bell. We'd better go on up. Mom really hates it when we're late for meals, though I suppose she won't get mad if you're here, since you're a guest."

I couldn't help smiling, and my heart warmed towards this lively little girl, in spite of my determination not to get sucked into any friendship with the MacDonald clan. I knew it might only lead to heartbreak later. It was bad enough that Bryan was so good-looking.

"We won't risk being late for lunch. Lead the way," I said and followed Amanda up the steep, winding flight, tree shadows alternating with flashes of sunlight on the water below. I stopped to catch my breath where a wide wooden deck led to the lower storey of the house.

The place was *huge*, and I suddenly felt afraid. Mom and I had talked about the lives of the rich and powerful in a casual sort of way, but I hadn't expected it to be quite like this. I had planned to worm my way into the lives and secrets of this family. Did I have the nerve to go ahead? I began to understand why the police had seemed to take so little interest in the MacDonalds thirty years ago.

Amanda was waiting for me at the top of the flight, where the wooden stairs led onto a spacious, south-facing deck to my right. Directly ahead of me a paved path widened to a forecourt where two cars were parked, a BMW sports car and a Mercedes coupe. *Typical*, I thought, picturing our ancient Volkswagen camper, which Dad was coaxing a few extra years out of. I tried not to be intimidated by it all and hurried to catch up.

The front door was wide open, and I caught a glimpse of a huge room running the full depth of the house, broken only by a massive free-standing stone fireplace. The far wall was all French windows; the sky and lake beyond were so dazzlingly bright that everything within seemed to be in deep shadow.

Out of the shadow came a tall, slender woman, in her mid-forties, I guessed. She was dressed casually in rough linen slacks and a shirt of raw silk, with a bright, expensive-looking scarf tucked into the neck. Her hair was dark and smoothly controlled in a short, neat cut. Her chunky earrings were obviously gold.

She held out her hand. "So you are Sandra. I am Margaret MacDonald, mother of these two scamps. Welcome to Treetops. I do hope you will enjoy your stay with us." The last words were gracious, but I couldn't help feeling that they were mechanical, that she had probably greeted a thousand guests with the same formula, in the same quiet voice.

Why should I be different? I scolded myself. *Did I expect her to jump up and down with joy? Amanda's warm welcome should be enough.*

"Thank you, Mrs. MacDonald. You're very kind. I hope Bryan didn't pressure you . . . I mean, is my staying with you really all right when you don't know me at all?"

Bryan's mother laughed and suddenly looked more friendly. "Of course it's all right. I am always happy to see my children's friends here. Away at boarding school for much of the year, they don't have many opportunities for making summertime friends. Now, Amanda will show you to the guest room and then we'll have lunch. I expect you're starving. I know Bry always is when he comes back—"

"The guest room! Oh, Mom, how awful! I quite forgot to tell you," Amanda wailed. "Uncle Greg phoned a while back. He said he was coming to stay."

"*What! Greg?* When?"

"This evening. I'm sorry, Mom."

"But he never . . . Amanda, *when* did he phone and exactly what did he say?"

"Just after Bry called. He said, 'How's things?' so I told him they were pretty boring, with Bry away most of the time. Then I said he was bringing a friend to stay— a diving buddy—and he started getting interested and asking all sorts of questions. Well, I didn't know the answers, and since Bry was away, I said, 'D'you want to talk to Mom?' and *he* said, 'No thanks. I don't need the annoyance. Just tell her that her favourite brother-in-law will be coming to stay.'"

"Did he say for how long? You *did* ask him that, didn't you?"

"Sure I did. He laughed and said, 'Let's just say it'll be an extended visit.'"

I was surprised to see Mrs. MacDonald flush at this news; she seemed more flustered than I would have expected. After all, I wasn't anyone important. She began to apologize. "I'm so sorry, Sandra. Really, it's too bad Amanda didn't pass on the message, though I suppose you and Bry would have been on your way here by then anyway." She hesitated, frowning.

"You don't have room for me, is that it?" I guessed. It seemed a ridiculous reason, however, given the size of the house.

"There *is* only the one guest room. 'An extended visit,' Greg said. Goodness knows what *that* means."

"Look, it's all right. I do understand." I tried to speak calmly, but I wanted to scream with frustration. Mom and Dad and I had spent so long planning, and I'd worked so hard to bring this visit about. Now, when success was within reach, was it going to be snatched away for a reason as stupid as no spare room?

"My parents won't be leaving till tomorrow," I went on. "If Bryan wouldn't mind taking me back this afternoon, I can just join up with them again."

"No, you've got to stay, Sandra." Amanda jumped up and down excitedly. "She can share my room, Mom, can't she? You won't mind sharing, will you, Sandra? There are two beds and I swear I don't snore."

I could have hugged Amanda. I looked at her mother. "Maybe having an extra person around will be a nuisance. If you don't see your brother-in-law that often . . ." My voice trailed away at the expression on Mrs. MacDonald's face. It was obvious that seeing Greg MacDonald was not high on her list of pleasurable events, and I realized that she had not been flustered by my arrival but by his visit.

"Nonsense. Amanda has solved the problem." She was once more the brisk, unflappable hostess. "That is, if *you* don't mind? Then that's wonderful. Amanda, take Sandra downstairs and get Bry to move her luggage from the guest room. Wait—is your room fit to be seen? You'd better make sure first. Show her the bathroom while you tidy it. And then come right up for lunch."

30

"Goody. Come on, Sandra." Amanda ran down a wide set of stairs to a small sitting room whose French windows looked out onto the lower deck. I glimpsed blue lake beyond the trees. A corridor to the left led to a series of doors, obviously the bedrooms. "This one's mine. Don't look! Here's the bathroom. Your towels are the pink ones. Don't come into the bedroom yet. I *do* need to do a bit of tidying."

The bathroom was as elegant as one in a four-star hotel, but with the charming addition of a large rubber duck and a toy frog with an appealing smile. When I'd washed up and combed my hair Amanda sent me upstairs again. "You can't come in yet. You mustn't look at the mess."

Alone at last, I looked curiously around the living room, taking in the oriental rugs on the polished floors, the comfortable-looking leather chairs and couches, and the low tables displaying the kind of expensive art objects that Mom and Dad sold in their boutique. A fieldstone fireplace bisected the space, separating living and dining areas. The vast dining table could seat, I guessed, a dozen or more. Then my eye was drawn from the fashionable interior to the expanse of blue sky, to the trees and the lake below. *Imagine living here every day*, I thought. *Would the view ever become common-place, or would every morning be a delight?* I found myself coveting not the house but the surroundings.

I walked through the open French windows onto the deck, which stretched the whole width of the house and looked to be over five metres deep. I peered down over the railing to the lower deck and into the trees. Cedars, maples and birch. The tangy scent of evergreens warmed by the sun drifted up. Out of sight below me were the dock and the boathouse. Beyond the trees the blueness of the lake vanished into a misty blur. Somewhere out there, between horizon and shore, was what I was seeking. My hands gripped the railing. Suddenly I wasn't envious any more. If Mom and I were right, there was a deadly serpent in this paradise.

"It's a wonderful view, isn't it? One I never tire of." Her voice behind me made me jump. I pulled myself together.

"It's gorgeous, Mrs. MacDonald."

"Do call me Margaret, my dear, or we'll get in a frightful muddle when my mother-in-law appears—too many MacDonalds altogether. Yes, Treetops is perfect on days like this. But there are times when storms come up suddenly, almost out of nowhere, and we have to batten down the hatches and cower indoors. Today, however, is certainly fine enough for eating on the deck. Do come and sit down. Oh, here is my husband. Don, this is Bryan's guest, Sandra Williams."

Donald MacDonald looked more as if he were in the military than stockbroking on Bay Street. Tight stomach, straight back, squared shoulders—as if he were on parade. He had Bryan's beaky nose, but his humourless mouth made him look severe and remote. *Not a friend*, I thought, and I was almost glad. The kindness of the MacDonalds was beginning to make me feel guilty—if they only knew why I was really here!

He shook my hand firmly, nodded briefly and sat down. "Where are the children, Margaret? I can't waste time. I've got a teleconference at precisely two."

"I don't know about Bryan, but Amanda's doing a fast cleanup of her room," I put in.

Mr. MacDonald frowned. "Why is she doing that now when we have a guest? Really, Margaret."

"Oh, Don, I meant to tell you. Amanda forgot to pass on the message. Greg's coming."

There was a sudden icy silence. It was as if the sun had gone behind a cloud. I looked at them curiously. Don MacDonald's face gave nothing away, but Margaret looked anxious and wasn't meeting his eyes. Then he frowned. "How long is he coming for?"

"He . . . he didn't say, Don. Anyway, Sandra has kindly offered to bunk in with Amanda."

"I suppose there's nothing we can do about it now." He shot out his wrist and consulted his watch. "Greg or no Greg, I must have my lunch immediately."

Margaret bustled indoors and came out with a tray of cold meats and salad.

"Anything I can help you with?" I asked, following her back into the kitchen.

"Thank you, dear. Plates and cutlery. Here we are. Napkins and rolls. Please go ahead while I call the children."

A moment later Amanda and Bryan hurried out. Their father looked at his watch again. He frowned, but said nothing.

"Sorry we're late, Dad," Bryan said cheerfully. "Things to do."

"So I hear. Mother's not coming up for lunch, Margaret?"

"You know she dislikes alfresco meals, so I took hers down to her sitting room." Margaret turned to me. "My mother-in-law has her own suite of rooms at the east end of the house, so she can be as independent as she wishes."

"And she's a very independent lady," Amanda added.

"I look forward to meeting her," I said politely. We

33

ate in silence until I turned to my host. "May I ask—do you work out of home? You were talking about a tele-conference."

"Most of the time I do. Nowadays there's little need for the frustration of commuting to a city office. We stay in town occasionally in winter, when the children are away at school—we have a condo—but my virtual office is just down the hall here." He glanced at his watch. "And I must be off. I will see you at dinner."

Once he had gone the atmosphere became consider-ably lighter. As soon as we'd finished I persuaded Bryan and Amanda to let me help with the clearing up.

"No dishwasher," Amanda warned. "Mom's ecologi-cally inclined."

I smiled at her serious, grown-up air. "All the more reason to do my share. I'll dry and one of you can put away, since I don't know where things go."

Once we'd finished Bryan said firmly, "I expect you'd like to unpack and get organized. Then, if you want to get into your swimming things, we'll do some snorkelling with Amanda."

Feeling rather as if I had been dismissed, I went downstairs and unpacked my few clothes. It didn't take long to hang up two dresses and fold my jeans and shirts away in the drawers provided. Then I changed into my navy Speedo and sandals, and went out through the bedroom's French window onto the deck outside. It was partially screened on either side, making a small private space. A padded lawn chair beckoned invitingly and I lay in the dappled sunshine, trying to relax.

"Okay, Amanda. Time to fess up." Bry's voice was

surprisingly close, and I realized with a start that the two must be in the room next door. "Exactly what did you say to Uncle Greg to bring him hotfooting it out here from town?"

"Nothing, really. Don't you bully me, Bry, or I'll . . . I'll . . ."

"Yes?"

"I'll tell Sandra what you're up to."

"You're bluffing, little sister. You don't have a clue."

"I do too! You've been desperate to find a diving buddy since your pal Mike backed out last summer."

"So?"

"So, if you want to know, that's what I told Uncle Greg. That you'd finally found someone. That you were bringing her over today and she'd be staying for ten days or so."

"What did he say to that?"

"Nothing. I mean there was this long silence and I thought we'd been cut off, so I said, 'Are you there, Uncle Greg?' and *he* said, 'You bet I am, and I'll be coming for an extended visit myself. Tell your mother to expect me early this evening, will you? I'm sure she'll be delighted.' Then he hung up."

I heard Bry give an impatient sigh. "You're a real pain, Amanda. Why'd you have to tell him about Sandra?"

"It's no big secret, is it? Nobody told *me* if it was. So get off my case, okay?"

I realized guiltily that I'd been listening to a very private conversation. I sat up and had just swung my legs down from the lawn chair when Bry spoke again. "Sorry, sprout. I should have warned you. But I never thought of Uncle Greg. He's a born troublemaker."

35

"That's okay. I'm sorry too if I've messed up. Maybe there's something I can do to help?"

"You can keep an eye on him for me. See what he's up to, especially when Sandra and I are diving."

"Like spying on him? Goody!"

"Only for goodness' sake don't make a big deal out of it, or he'll get suspicious. Now go see if she's ready, will you?"

I slipped back into the bedroom and quietly closed the door behind me. When Amanda burst into the room, I was standing by the mirror, brushing my hair.

"Sorry I kept you waiting, Sandra. I'll just jump into my suit and we'll go down."

"No problem." I managed a casual smile, struggling with an uncomfortable mixture of guilt and curiosity. What was the problem with Uncle Greg?

I suppose it should have been a great afternoon, swimming and snorkelling in the little bay with Amanda and Bryan, but to me it seemed a waste of time. I wanted to get out into deep water, to do some serious scuba diving. To find out what was driving Bryan. So far I'd had no hint. Just that he desperately needed a diving partner. For what? I could guess, but I didn't *know*.

Eventually we climbed the steps up to the lower-floor deck. "This way, we don't get water and sand on Mom's precious rugs," Amanda explained, and we were just deciding who should have the first shower when we heard the high-pitched whine of a fast car coming down the driveway above us.

"Shoot. That's Uncle Greg." Amanda frowned. "I'd recognize his MG anywhere. I was hoping he'd get held up and not arrive till after dinner."

36

"Not your favourite uncle, I guess?"

"Uh-uh. Too bad he's the only uncle we've got."

"Any particular reason for your dislike?"

"Wait till you meet him. You'll find out."

This sounded ominous, so when I had showered, washed my hair and changed into one of my two dresses, I went upstairs somewhat cautiously. The notorious Uncle Greg was standing alone in the living room, a tall slender man with hair a shade darker than Bryan and Amanda's, smoothed back from a well-shaped head. His cheekbones were high and his nose straight and thin, his eyes grey. He might have looked as severe as his brother but for his lips, which were well shaped and full. He was wearing navy slacks, a light blue silk shirt and a blazer with a crest on the pocket.

"So you're Bry's diving buddy. Well, well. Amanda never divulged your sex. Very nice indeed." He took my hand, and idiotically I found myself glad I'd chosen to wear the blue-green dress that made my eyes look green instead of vaguely hazel. He went on looking at me and I found my cheeks getting hot as I told him my name. "Very nice indeed," he repeated. He was still holding my hand, and I began to feel really uncomfortable.

I was wondering how to get my hand back without appearing rude when Don MacDonald came out of his office. "So you've arrived, Greg."

"Indeed. Turning up like a bad penny, dear brother, and thirsting for a drink. Oh, Margaret. Lovely to see you, my dear. All the more for knowing my taste in drinks."

"A dry martini, I believe, Greg." She handed a cocktail to her brother-in-law and one to her husband. "Some fruit juice for you, Sandra?"

"Thank you, that'll be great."

"Will Mother be joining us for dinner?" Greg asked.

"Yes, indeed. A celebration, with all of us here. And our young guest." Margaret's smile was icy and I wondered if *my* presence, as well as Greg's, had upset her. There was an awkward silence, broken by the appearance of the elder Mrs. MacDonald, Bryan and Amanda's grandmother, in a drift of chiffon scarves.

Vague and fluffy was my first impression as we shook hands. But then I was startled by a very searching look from the sharp blue eyes and changed my mind. Someone to reckon with after all. What with her and the too-curious Uncle Greg, I realized that I would have to be on my guard.

Dinner in the dining room, with rows of knives and forks, damask napkins and wineglasses, was served unobtrusively by Amanda and her mother. "We used to have live-in staff, but it was too difficult. They all hated the remoteness. So now I just have a woman who comes in three times a week to keep the dust and cobwebs at bay," Margaret explained.

Soup was followed by stuffed lake trout, and Greg made a sarcastic remark about dressing for dinner in the jungle. His mother retorted, "Hardly jungle, my dear. It's only thirty kilometres to the nearest supermarket."

I soon noticed that Greg enjoyed needling his family. In one form or another throughout the meal came small poisonous jabs, aimed at one or another of them—and even me.

It was Amanda who innocently started him off. "Why does your luggage have the initials CW on it, when your name's Sandra Williams? Are you a secret agent or something?"

There was a curious silence, and I had the uneasy feeling that someone at the table was waiting for my answer, as if it were important. I laughed. "Nothing so romantic. Actually, my real first name is a deep, dark secret."

"Oh, please tell," Amanda begged. "I warn you, I'm a madly curious person. I'll get it out of you somehow."

"Amanda, watch your manners," her mother said reprovingly.

"It's all right, Margaret." I relented. "Actually it's Cassandra, but I really don't like owning up to it."

"Cassandra. But that's a very pretty name. Don't you think so, Bry?" Amanda turned to him.

Before Bryan could answer, Greg interrupted, his eyes gleaming with mischief. "Oh, no, Amanda. It's not pretty at all. It's a name filled with foreboding. Cassandra was a woman in ancient Greece who knew the truth when nobody else did, and the truth was always bad news. Isn't that right, Cassandra?"

While I was still hunting for the right reply, Margaret got to her feet and said crossly, "Do stop being such a bore, Greg, and help clear the plates while I bring in dessert."

This verbal sniping was making me increasingly uncomfortable, and as soon as the meal was over I jumped up and volunteered to do the dishes. "But you are our guest," Margaret protested half-heartedly, but then with a "thank you, child," she swept her husband, mother-in-law and Greg off to play bridge.

"Lucky for you I'm here to make a foursome," Greg said smugly, and was squashed by his brother, who snapped, "We do very well playing three-handed cut-throat bridge most evenings, thank you."

"Whew!" Amanda blew out an expressive sigh when we were safely in the kitchen. "Glad that's over. Wow! Look at this kitchen! Mom's made a worse mess than usual. Happens when she gets really creative. Okay, let's get the show on the road. Bry, you get to wash this time."

Once the dishes were done and put away, the counters scrubbed down and the towels hung up, I followed the others into the living room. Amanda went immediately to a closet hidden in the wood-panelled wall, which opened to reveal a dozen board games. "Let me choose, Bry, please. Monopoly, okay?"

Bryan groaned.

"Oh, *please*. It'll be much more fun with three of us. You're so predictable, Bry, but Sandra's an unknown quantity. You *do* like Monopoly, don't you, Sandra?"

I meekly agreed, though I hadn't played it since about grade six, when I hadn't much enjoyed it. I soon realized why Bryan had groaned. Amanda had uncanny luck with the dice, and before long her hotels were trapping us round after round.

"I'll declare bankruptcy in a moment," Bryan warned.

Their father, who was dummy, had wandered over to look at the board. Now he chuckled. "Attagirl. You take after me. Don't let him cry off without a fight."

"You bet I won't, Dad. You can sell me—um—States Avenue and St. Charles Place, Bry."

"They're not worth enough to get me out of the hole."

"So why did you buy them in the first place?"

"Because I'm dumb, dumb, dumb, little sister. Now are you satisfied?"

I groaned. "And she already owns the Electric Company—three more properties in a row."

Don MacDonald chuckled. "She'll be a business woman one day." He rumpled her hair.

"Not if it involves math, Dad. Anyway I've decided I'm going to be a marine biologist and save the environment."

"You just borrowed that ambition from me, Amanda," I retorted.

"Saving the environment?" Don MacDonald smiled.

I laughed. "More modestly, I just hope to go to Dalhousie University and study marine biology. Then I'll get to spend the rest of my life diving and getting paid for it."

"Diving?" His voice was suddenly sharp.

"Didn't you know, Don? Your guest is going to be exploring these waters with Bry. Diving buddies, they call them. That's what her visit to Treetops is all about." There was no mistaking the jab in Greg's voice—nor the stony expression I suddenly saw on Don MacDonald's face.

No one spoke. Then, "Come on, you two," Grandmother MacDonald called across the room. "Time for another rubber before bed. Don't dawdle."

Trying to relax that night in yet another unfamiliar bed, I thought thankfully of getting out of the house tomorrow, of diving, far removed from these disturbingly quarrelsome adults. And the beginning of *my* search, I promised myself.

But the next morning I awoke to a brilliant red sunrise and a sky covered with curdled clouds like cottage cheese. The wind was rising, and by the time breakfast was over the sky had darkened ominously and the lake was heaving with slow, sullen waves.

"Well, that's it for today. Maybe tomorrow," Bryan said regretfully. "This could be a doozer of a storm."

"No diving? What a waste. I'd been . . ." I bit back the rest of my words. *To be so close . . .*

"Not really a waste, Sandra. It'll give me a chance to tell you what I'm planning. Come on."

"For our dives? You've got something special in mind? Now I *am* curious." I followed him downstairs.

"Me too? Please, Bry?" Amanda hung over the railing.

"No way, Amanda. You're too young. Come on, Sandra."

He led me into his room and closed the door. I felt a second's worry, then told myself that it was ridiculous. He knew nothing of my plans. And if he did, what could he do? Nothing could happen to me here, not in a house full of people. He gave me a quizzical look that seemed to my guilty mind to say, *I know exactly what you're thinking.* Then he opened the French window leading onto the lower deck and stepped outside.

The wind surged in, blowing the curtains violently back into the room. The rain was already bucketing down, and I instinctively drew back from the onslaught of the storm. But then I saw that even with the wind blowing from the southwest, we were partly sheltered from the rain by the overhanging deck above.

"Come on." Bryan urged me outside. The temperature had dropped dramatically and I wrapped my arms around my body and shivered.

"Why do we have to stand out here?"

He held up one hand. "Listen. Just listen."

I listened to the wind and waves, to tree branches

creaking and groaning. To the rain hissing down through the leaves, splattering on the deck. I shrugged and looked at Bryan. "Noisy, isn't it!"

"No, you're not doing it right. You've got to listen *through* the storm." His face was intense, his eyes earnest. He seemed suddenly older than the carefree young man I'd met two days ago.

I tried to do as he said. *How do you listen through a racket like this?* And then I did hear it. And once I heard it, I wondered how I'd missed noticing it before. It was a muffled sound, uneven but distinct. The tolling of a distant bell. *Dong! Dong! Dong!* I shivered.

His eyes were on my face. "What do you think it is?"

"A bell buoy," I guessed. "Storm warning?"

He shook his head.

"A ship's bell?" I remembered the wreck we'd explored outside the harbour and shivered again. *A bell like that?* I thought, and hoped my expression didn't give away my family's secret knowledge. "I wouldn't want to be out in a storm like this," I said lightly. "Will it make harbour safely?"

He shook his head again. "It's not a passing ship. We hear this bell every time the storm comes from the southwest."

"But that's just not possible. It's not a buoy. Not a passing ship. Why, you make it sound like—" I laughed nervously, though it wasn't in the least funny—"like a ghost bell!"

Bryan said nothing, but I could feel his reaction like an electric current between us. I stood transfixed, listening. *Dong! Dong!* A bell tolling for the dead. I remembered hearing about a ship that sank in Lake Winnipeg, whose bell could be heard tolling from beneath the waves during storms. But that had been a merchant ship, not a yacht.

The spell was broken by the sudden crash of music coming from inside the house, and I jumped. Wagner, I guessed, at his stormiest. Bryan turned and gestured to me to come indoors again. As he closed the French window, the noise of the storm was quenched and Wagner thundered even more loudly against my eardrums.

"Wow, that's loud!"

"Quite something, isn't it? Dad always plays that recording during a storm. He says it helps him concentrate."

"*Concentrate?* I don't believe it!"

"No, of course not. He plays it to hide the sound of the bell."

I stared at Bryan. "Why? What does the bell mean to him? Though I admit it's spooky."

"The wreck of *Far Skimmer* is out there. She foundered on a shoal and sank."

My heart skipped a beat. Again the familiar name . . . *Be cool*, I told myself. *Remember, you know nothing.* "Your father's yacht?"

"Grandfather's. She capsized when Dad and Uncle Greg were sailing with him. Thirty years ago, when they were just kids."

"But yachts don't have ships' bells, do they? I thought only merchant vessels had them, to mark the watches."

Bryan shrugged. "I guess it was a fancy of Grandfather's. The bell was an antique he found, and he had his yacht's name engraved on it."

"You're saying that the bell's been ringing ever since?

44

Weird. But you'd think your dad would be used to it by now."

"Uh-uh. Dad sold our house in Toronto and moved out here after Grandfather died and left Treetops to him. That was maybe four years ago. It was then I noticed Dad and Uncle Greg having really serious fights. Oh, they'd never got on, but the arguments became a lot worse. Uncle Greg came to stay whenever he was short of money." Bryan's face reddened. "I shouldn't be talking about that. It has nothing to do with with what's going on really. But that's when we began to hear the bell, maybe a couple of years ago. *Far Skimmer* must have shifted in a storm, I guess. Dad got more and more edgy. He won't talk about it. He's never talked about the day *Far Skimmer* was wrecked. He just shuts himself in his office and plays loud music whenever there's a big storm coming in from the southwest. It makes Mom miserable, but he won't talk to her about the wreck either."

"What about your grandmother? Haven't you ever asked her why he reacts this way?"

Bryan shook his head. "I tried once and she got very grandmotherish and told me not to interfere in things that weren't my business."

"Not much fun. But why are you telling me all this? What's it got to do with our dives?" I dropped into an armchair and wrapped my arms around my knees so he wouldn't see my hands shake. I took a deep breath and tried to appear calm. What I'd been waiting to hear was *so* close.

"Okay. Once I overheard Dad say to Grandmother, 'That damn bell. If only I didn't have to listen to that damn bell.' That's when I decided to look for *Far*

Skimmer. I want to dive till I find her and bring back that bell. Then maybe Dad will be free of whatever's bugging him, and our family will be the way it used to be."

chapter THREE

I MUST have been holding my breath. Now I let it out in a huge sigh. Bryan was only looking for the bell. That was all. He had no idea . . . But his plan was going to lead me straight to *Far Skimmer*. This was better than I'd ever dreamed it could be. Much better.

As these thoughts flashed through my mind, I saw him looking at me, waiting for some response, and I managed to answer. "But the lake's so big. How do you ever expect to find her?"

"I thought about it all last winter, and I've narrowed it down to three likely areas. So that's what I want to do, with your help—explore those three places." He dropped to his knees and opened the blanket drawer under his bed. "I keep my charts here so I don't have to roll them," he explained.

He took out a chart and laid it on top of his desk, pushing aside books and a pen tray. I got up and looked over his shoulder. I had pored over a lot of maps of this lake since I'd been told the family tragedy, but I pretended ignorance. "So what are all these lines and numbers? It looks more like a weather map than a chart of the lake."

"It's the same principle, only instead of linking isobars of the same pressure, the way weather maps do, the lines link places of the same depth. The numbers are soundings measured in fathoms. Any particular hazards, like shoals or known wrecks, are also marked, often with buoys. Like here and here." He pointed to several places on the map.

"How come *Far Skimmer* isn't marked?"

"Because nobody knows where she went down."

"Surely your grandfather did?"

Bryan shook his head. "All he could tell them was the course they were on before the storm got really bad, and how far they'd sailed up to that point. After that, I suppose time and direction were a blur."

"And the boys, your father and your uncle Greg? Were they asked?"

"They only confirmed what little my grandfather could tell the authorities. Just that they were aiming for home, but visibility was so bad they couldn't see the buoys. Then they struck a shoal."

"Like this?" I pointed to the long reef running diagonally across the chart, now and then coming close to the surface. "That covers a lot of territory."

"It sure does. But I've figured out the possibilities." From the drawer Bryan pulled out several sheets of tracing paper and laid one of them on top of the chart, matching up the features carefully. "This dotted line shows the most likely course of *Far Skimmer*. I've marked the areas where the reef is closest to the surface, where she would most likely have run onto it. But you can see how well this particular area is marked with buoys. Why didn't Grandfather see them, even in a storm? I've been out myself in all but the worst weather, and I don't see how he could have missed them. Which leaves *this* spot and *this* one as possible wreck sites." He indicated two arcs marked in red.

My heart was thudding so loudly I thought he'd hear it. I took a deep breath and tried to speak casually. "It all sounds a bit iffy. Suppose we find nothing?"

"Then we move on to Plan B." He whipped off the

sheet of tracing paper and replaced it with another. "Could be between here and here. If that's no go, I *do* have Plan C, though it seems less likely. It all depends on how much *Far Skimmer* was driven off course. And we know she's shifted a bit. She must have shifted two years ago because that's when we started hearing the bell."

"Impressive research," I said as calmly as I could. I could feel my heart beating almost out of control and the adrenalin rising. "So your idea is to explore the first site as soon as the weather clears?"

"Weather *and* water. No point trying to explore while there's a lot of sediment about."

"But the bottom is mainly limestone, isn't it? Shouldn't it clear up quite fast?"

Bryan put the charts back in the drawer and looked up at me, a sparkle in his eyes. "Hey, you sound as keen as I am."

I managed a laugh. "It's like a treasure hunt, isn't it? You find the ship, grab the bell and bring it home. You're sure that's what your father wants?"

"Sure I'm sure. Remember what he said to my grandmother?"

"Okay. But why is your scheme a secret? Your father and Greg might have more memories about the wreck—ones that didn't surface at the time but have since. Memories that might help you find the yacht."

He shook his head. "The wreck of *Far Skimmer* has always been a forbidden subject. We don't talk about it—ever. Or the bell. Or Father's bursts of Wagner during storms."

"Not even your uncle Greg?"

"What d'you mean?"

"Well, it's obvious that he really enjoys needling your dad. Doesn't *he* ever talk about the wreck?"

"I see what you mean. No, it's never mentioned, not when we're around anyway. But I'm sure the memory's always there, buried just under the surface."

"Under the lake. Why *is* Greg here, do you think?"

Bryan looked at me in surprise. "But you heard why. Because Amanda told him you were coming."

"Specifically she told him that we were planning *dives*. That was when he got interested. Don't you see?"

"You think he came to find out what we're up to? That he suspects I'm interested in *Far Skimmer*? I wonder if you're right. That'd be a real pain. I want the bell to be a surprise." He gave an impatient sigh. "Amanda should never have told him I'd found a diving buddy. Stupid."

"How was she to know?" I argued. "I think you're making a great mistake not letting her in on your plans."

"But she's just an eleven-year-old kid. She'd tell every-one."

"Eleven going on twelve, she says. Nonsense, Bryan. She's as smart as a whip. She told Greg about my coming here only because she *didn't* know the diving was supposed to be a secret."

"Hmm. Maybe you're right." He brooded silently for a minute, then uncurled himself from the floor and went out into the corridor. "You there, kid?"

"Yeah. Dad's so-called music's driving me crazy. How come I'm not allowed to play *my* discs that loud?"

"Because the world is unfair to kids. Come on in. I've got something to tell you, if you promise never to tell a living soul."

50

In bed that night I found myself smiling at the memory of Amanda's face, her eyes growing rounder and rounder as Bryan explained his plans.

"I'll never tell anybody, even if . . . if they pull out my fingernails with red-hot pincers."

"Where do you get such gruesome ideas? I hardly think Uncle Greg will resort to torture," Bryan retorted.

"Maybe not. But I certainly don't trust him." Amanda nodded wisely. "So you watch out, Sandra. Uncle Greg is creepy."

I woke early the next morning, my mind homing in on our planned dive. Was the weather co-operating? I tiptoed to the window and drew back the drape. Perfect! Through the dancing leaves I could see flashes of blinding sun on the lake. In the other bed Amanda lay in a tangle of bedclothes. Impulsively I pulled on my swimsuit, pushed my feet into sandals, grabbed a towel and slipped out of the French window onto the deck outside our room.

Raindrops still hung from the leaves in the canopy above, and now and then as I went down the steps, one would spill its load of icy water onto my back and shoulders. But the sun was already hot, busily sucking up moisture into swirls of mist that eddied between the trees and drifted across the surface of the lake.

I dropped my towel on the dock and dived into the lake. It was still choppy and far colder than I'd expected and I rose to the surface gasping and shaking the hair out of my eyes. Wow! The water felt as if that storm had come out of the Arctic. I stroked swiftly away from the dock, swimming fast to get the heat back into my body.

Then I turned and swam parallel to the shore, to and fro, until I figured I'd covered a couple of kilometres.

Back on the dock I spread my towel on the warm planks and lay on my back to catch my breath, my eyes closed against the dazzle of the sun. I was beginning to think fondly of breakfast—was that the smell of coffee and bacon wafting down from the house?—when a shadow fell across me. "That you, Bryan?"

"Who do you think, Cassandra?" a voice mocked me. My eyes flew open. It was Greg looming over me. He dropped to the dock beside me. "Cassandra, prophet of ill omen," he went on. "Is that what you really are? Have you come among us to bring evil tidings? Wars and the rumours of war." His voice was light, but something about his manner gave me gooseflesh. What had Amanda said yesterday? "You watch out. Uncle Greg is creepy." *She's only a kid*, I thought. *But sometimes children see the truth more clearly than adults.*

I propped myself up on one elbow, wishing he were not sitting quite so close. "You know perfectly well I'm just spending a couple of weeks with Bryan and Amanda. My foolish name has nothing to do with it. And I *really* prefer Sandra, if you don't mind."

"But Cassandra seems so much more appropriate, don't you agree?"

I didn't answer, willing him to go away, but he sat staring across the lake, his hands linked around his knees.

"So what's your opinion of older men?" The question was so unexpected that I stared at him. Was that a joke or a come-on? But the sun was still so low, dancing across the water, that he was silhouetted against its shifting light and I couldn't see his expression. The scent of his pungent aftershave, artificial against the clean smell of water and pine, made my nostrils wrinkle. I said nothing.

"You must have an opinion one way or another," he persisted.

"Why should I?"

"Because you are a young woman of strong opinions, I would guess."

"Sure, I have opinions. And prejudices too. But not necessarily about older men in general. My opinions are more personal than that, and they are my own, and I don't have to share them unless I choose," I snapped. *All he wants is to winkle the truth out of me—why I'm here, what Bryan is planning. No way!*

He was sitting on the edge of my towel, making it impossible for me to get up, wrap it around me and escape up the steps. But I couldn't stand being near him another minute. I swung my legs over the edge of the dock and swam out into the lake. A few minutes later, thinking longingly about a hot shower and a good breakfast, I turned and looked back. He had gone. Thankfully I made for the shore, wrapped the towel around me and ran up to the house.

Warm and dressed, I discovered Amanda in the kitchen, making pancakes. "That smells wonderful. Count me in."

"You sure can swim. Wasn't the water icy? It usually is after a storm."

"Pretty cold. But I feel great now. Is Bryan up yet?"

"No. It's still quite early though."

I looked up at the kitchen clock. "Seven-fifteen. Good grief! Did I wake you?"

"Uh-uh. I'm usually the first one up. Breakfast is my

53

specialty. I can even do eggs Benedict, though poaching the eggs is pretty tricky."

"I much prefer pancakes. Your uncle Greg was up very early too. Down by the dock."

"Admiring the view, I suppose?" Amanda said in such a put-on grown-up voice that I burst out laughing. The tension inside me dissolved. Stupid to be upset by such an unimportant incident. So I managed to keep my cool when I followed Amanda out onto the deck with her stack of pancakes and found Greg already there, smoking one of his foreign cigarettes.

"Good morning," I said coolly, as if we had not already met.

"Pancakes! For me?" He reached out for the plate Amanda was carrying. She snatched it away from him. "Go make your own, Uncle Greg. There's a pitcher of mix by the stove. Come on, Sandra. Dig in." She sat down and spread butter and maple syrup lavishly over her pile.

I followed suit. "I hope we're not planning to dive right away," I joked, my mouth full. "With this load of pancakes I'd sink like a stone."

Amanda shook her head and swallowed. "That's why Bry's sleeping in, I bet. The water'll be too cloudy for a while. No fun."

Greg turned from the railing, tossing his cigarette into the brush. "Why don't I take you for a drive along the coast, Sandra? We'll find a nice place for lunch and make a day of it. What do you say?"

I flashed a plea for help towards Amanda, who quickly intervened. "We've already got plans for the day, Uncle Greg."

"Suit yourself." He shrugged and went indoors.

Shortly afterwards he appeared again, a blazer slung over his shoulders. "Sure you won't change your mind? I can promise you a much more interesting day than you'll have with these two."

"No, thanks." I shook my head and he went out the front door. Bryan was just coming out onto the deck as we heard Greg gunning his engine and roaring up the driveway to the road.

"He's out of the way? Good."

"But it isn't important, is it? Amanda said we wouldn't be diving for a while, after the storm."

Bryan cocked an eyebrow at his sister. "Huh?"

"I only said that to put him off," she explained.

"You mean we *will* be diving? That's great!"

"We're only going snorkelling. Just to look over the first site."

"Great. That means I can come too." Amanda bounced up and down.

"Well, I guess maybe we'll let you." Bryan pretended to sound reluctant, and his sister danced around the table and hugged him.

"For that I'll make your pancakes too."

Later, with wetsuits on, we took *Moonlight* out onto the lake. Once we were past the islands I noticed a small chop on the water, the tail end of yesterday's storm, but the sky was cloudless and there was very little wind.

When Bryan cut the engine we heard only the small sounds of waves slapping against the hull. "How can you tell this is the right place?" I asked as he dropped the anchor over the bow.

"I've got a fix on the two buoys over there." He pointed.

"I can see only one. . . oh, now I see the other just behind it."

"Exactly. That gives us a straight line. But to get an intersection I need two other markers. One is the point to the west of our bay, and the other is that rock in front."

"Two intersected lines. So X marks the spot?"

"Hope so. Keep your fingers crossed. I've moored us so we'll be exploring against the current and tide. Then when we're swimming back to *Moonlight*, we'll have them to help us. D'you want to put on your mask and fins now, Sandra?"

"Why not me first? Please, Bry," Amanda pleaded.

"I need you to be lookout. Don't worry, sprout, you'll get your turn. Come on, Sandra."

I followed him over the side, cleared my snorkel and waved to Amanda. Then I set out beside Bryan, an arm's length away from him, scanning the depths from just below the surface. The bottom was clearly defined, with the reef falling away into the fading colours of the depths on our left. At the sight of a bulky shadow we both dived, but it was only a huge boulder, perhaps dumped in the lake during the last ice age.

We surfaced, blew our snorkels clear and swam on until Bryan signalled for us to turn. This time we scanned the offshore side of the shoal, moving slowly through the water, constantly looking below us to right and left. Back at *Moonlight* I pulled off my fins, tossed them aboard and climbed up the stern steps.

"Any luck?" Amanda asked eagerly.

I took off my mask and tried not to show my disappointment. "Just some interesting marine life. Lots of fish—some biggish perch and a school of rock bass—but that's all."

56

"Let me try, Bry. Maybe I'll see something you missed."

"We'll move to a new position first." He pulled up the anchor, started the engine and let the boat chug slowly along. "Tell me if the two buoys get out of line, will you, Amanda?"

"A bit to port, Bry. Okay. That's it."

A few hundred metres farther along the shoal he stopped the engine again and dropped the anchor. "This will do. Will you keep lookout, Sandra?"

"Sure. What am I looking out for?"

"Just to make sure that any passing boat notices our diving flag and stays well away."

Alone, I settled comfortably on the upper deck and looked around. There was nothing in sight except for a few white dots of sails far out on the lake. I could see Bryan and Amanda just below the surface. They dived and then surfaced, cleared their snorkels and swam on. I looked around again and was suddenly dazzled by a flash of light from the landward side. The sun on the windshield of a passing car? The main road around the lake must be somewhere along there, though I couldn't see it through the trees.

There it was again. Right in my eyes. Coming from the same place, so it probably wasn't a car. A cottage window catching the sun? I stared and then blinked as I was blinded once more. This time I was positive that the light was coming from the headland to the east of Treetops. Only, as far as I knew, there was nothing out there but bush.

I turned my head away, my brain working overtime. Binoculars, trained on the boat, on *me*, I guessed. It had to be. Casually I looked out across the lake in the opposite direction, shading my eyes, acting out for whoever the secret watcher was that I hadn't noticed him, that I had no idea I was being spied upon. By the time Bryan and Amanda had made their way back to the boat and climbed aboard, I had already made up my mind not to mention the incident. Not yet. Maybe I was only imagining that it was of any importance. *But I will see if there's a trail from the house to that head-land*, I promised myself as we chugged back to shore.

Amanda was discouraged. "I don't see how we'll ever find her. The lake is so huge and empty."

But Bryan didn't seem worried. "That was just Plan A," he said as he led the way up the hill, whistling cheerfully. Once we had showered and changed, he laid the second piece of tracing paper over his chart. "It's anyone's guess which way the wind was blowing at the moment she hit the shoal. In a bad storm the wind can blow all round the compass. And the tides and winds may have shifted her since, of course. Anyway, this is my next best guess."

"Can we check Plan B this afternoon?" Amanda asked eagerly.

"Sure. Once we've digested lunch. An hour or so, okay?"

The break gave me the chance to sneak away. I strolled nonchalantly around the house to the east of the driveway. The wilderness had been allowed to grow quite close to the house, and I kept my eyes peeled for an opening along the edge of the lawn that might turn into a path.

I nearly missed it. It was almost invisible in the grass, but a footprint at the edge of a puddle left from yesterday's storm gave me the clue. I stepped over the puddle and, beyond a clump of fern, found a faint trail winding among the trees. At some time in the past the brush had obviously been cleared, though not for a few years, I guessed. I skirted a patch of poison ivy and walked slowly on. The trees thinned. Suddenly a small, rocky promontory in front of me dropped abruptly several metres to the lake below. From this spot I could see clearly past the small inshore islets to the place where we'd been diving. Someone could have stood just here, watching us.

I was about to turn back when I saw two cigarette stubs ground into the wet turf. Unusual cigarettes, oval-shaped rather than round—foreign cigarettes. Greg's. Since they were perfectly dry, they must have been dropped there this morning, after the storm. Greg had left, saying he was going for a drive. We'd heard him go, but he could easily have parked up on the road and come back on foot. I quickly retraced my steps to the front of the house. The BMW and the Mercedes were there, but Greg's red MG was still gone.

I hurried down the steps leading to the lower deck, kicked off my muddy shoes and went into the house. Amanda was waiting in her swimsuit.

"We're all ready for another dive. Bry's gone down to the dock. Where did you vanish to?"

"I'll tell you later." *Maybe I can trust you and Bryan,* I thought. *But who else? Not Don MacDonald, surrounded by computers and fax machines, playing Wagner to blot out the sound of a bell. What about Margaret? Always elegantly dressed, running the house like a northern Martha Stewart. Is there more to her than that? Even Grandmother MacDonald—does she know, or suspect, what happened thirty years ago?*

59

"I'll tell you when we're out on the water, with no eavesdroppers," I promised.

"Goody, a secret!" Amanda gave a wriggle of excitement. Then a shadow crossed her face and she looked a little lost. "Something's wrong, isn't there?"

I hadn't realized I was so transparent. *I must be more careful*, I reminded myself. I tried to smile reassuringly. "Probably nothing but my fevered imagination. Sorry to have kept you waiting. I'll just jump into my suit."

A few minutes later, with wetsuits over our swimsuits, carrying our snorkels and masks, we went along the dock to the launch. "Second site this afternoon. Keep your fingers crossed," Bryan said as he started the engine.

"Suppose we find nothing there?" Amanda asked anxiously.

"We still have Plan C. After that we'll go back to the first site and scuba dive in the deeper water for the whole length of the reef. But that's a really time-consuming way of going about it. I'd rather know where we're looking before we get into serious diving."

"Well, let's not borrow trouble." I managed to look cheerful, far from what I was feeling. "But talking of trouble . . ." I told them what I had seen that morning and how I'd confirmed my guess that Greg had been spying on us. "It must have been this morning. The ground was still wet, but his footprints—and his smelly cigarette stubs—were fresh."

"But we all heard him drive away at breakfast time," Amanda objected.

"Easy enough for him to park up on the road, wait until we were out on the water and then slip back. But why?" Bryan frowned.

"Because he's a slime," Amanda said.

"That's not a reason. That's just prejudice, Amanda. What do you think, Sandra?"

The truth shall make you free, someone had once said. Would it set us free this time? Maybe Mom's terrible suspicions were unfounded. Maybe not. But if she was right, I was sure Greg was involved. There was only one way to find out. "We need to find *Far Skimmer* as soon as we can. And . . ." I hesitated. "If we *do* get lucky, let's not signal our success. Maybe Greg's back on the headland, watching us. No, don't look now, Amanda. On the other hand, don't *not* look. I mean, just act naturally."

Bryan steered the launch to his second choice of possible sites and anchored. As before, he and I made the first dive. As before, we swam below the surface, scanning the shadowy depths as far as possible. Again we saw the sharp edge of the limestone, the fishes darting to and fro, the occasional shadows that made my heart jump but turned out to be nothing more than loose chunks of limestone.

We went back to the launch, and Bryan and Amanda searched in the other direction. Again there was nothing. "Never mind," I said, trying to cheer Amanda up. "Tomorrow's another day. We'll give Bryan's third site a try."

"And suppose we don't find anything there?" she wailed.

"Like I said before, sprout," Bryan told her, "Sandra and I will go back and scuba dive over the whole area if we have to. A lot more work, but we'll manage."

It has been four days since Bryan asked me here. Let's hope we get lucky tomorrow. We could spend weeks combing the depths—and I don't have weeks.

We felt a sense of pressure now, and the next morning we were up early and out after a quick breakfast of orange juice, cereal and toast. Bryan and I had been swimming for about five minutes when we both saw a dark shadow below us. We filled our lungs and kicked our way down. Bryan fumbled at his belt and found the switch on his flashlight.

As if by magic the greys of our surroundings were transformed. I saw the reef rising above us on our left, speckled rock covered with green seaweed. Schools of rock bass, rainbow coloured, shimmered to and fro. Just below us was the stern of what must once have been a handsome yacht. Still faintly visible was the name: *Far Skimmer*.

We rose to the surface and greedily sucked in fresh air. Then we swam back to the launch and climbed aboard. Bryan was grinning from ear to ear. I had no idea what I looked like—my emotions were so mixed. The triumphant end of a quest—or the beginning of horror?

"You weren't gone long. You've found her! You did it! I can tell by your faces—"

"Hold on, Amanda," I interrupted. "Has he been watching?"

"I think so. I caught a flash. After that I pretended not to notice, the way you said."

"Good. Let's keep up the pretence. Suppose we hadn't found anything, what would we do now?"

"Dive again. That way." Bryan pointed. "You're right, Sandra. We've got to keep him guessing." He pulled up the anchor and moved the launch eastward. "Want to dive, Amanda?"

"I guess so. Though it isn't much fun when you've already found her."

"Never mind. Pretend you're an actress doing a scene. Lights! Camera! Away we go, putting Uncle Greg off the scent."

"*All right!*"

Alone on the launch I did my part, acting out my pretended frustration, watching the progress of the snorkellers, looking at my watch, then out at the lake. Finally I slumped onto the padded seat in the stern and gazed abstractedly at nothing. But my mind was working furiously.

The wreck wasn't too deep. It lay in no more than sixty feet of water on the landward slope of the shoal on which it had been wrecked. A couple of dives should finally give me the answer I'd been waiting for ever since Mom had shared her suspicions with me. Soon it would be over. Soon I could stop acting my part and go home. But the worst was still ahead. I licked my lips and swallowed, suddenly afraid of what I might find.

chapter FOUR

"NOT A PEEP out of you at lunchtime," Bryan warned Amanda as we went upstairs after showering and changing.

"Of course not. Don't you trust me, Bry?" Her lip trembled, though I saw that her eyes were dancing with excitement.

I couldn't help smiling at her display of wounded innocence. "Sure he trusts you, Amanda. But could you dim your lights just a little? You're practically incandescent!"

"Huh?"

"Sandra means that you look as if it's your birthday and you've just been given a pony."

"Don't I wish! Okay, I'll concentrate on thinking about the pony I know I'm *never* going to get. There, is that better?"

We were still laughing at her woebegone expression as we went into the kitchen to help ourselves from the array of luncheon meats, cheeses, bread and fruit that Margaret had spread out on the counter. Don had already taken his lunch out to the deck, and Greg joined us while we were filling our plates. I felt a sudden shiver, as if his very presence lowered the temperature. Why was he spying on us? His face was smooth, his expression blandly friendly.

I was giving him a few covert glances as I served myself when he looked up and stared at me coldly. I quickly turned away and took my lunch out onto the deck. It was his eyes, I realized, that made me uneasy. Even when his lips widened in a smile, his grey eyes remained cold and expressionless.

In a sudden flash of memory I was four years old again. I had tripped on a paving stone leading up to the house and had dropped my favourite doll—that had belonged to my great-aunt—shattering its china head to pieces. But what had given me nightmares for weeks was the sight of the two blue glass eyes, still attached to each other by the mechanism that made them open and shut, rolling out onto the path and staring blankly up at me.

How absurd to remember that, I thought, rubbing my arms, which were suddenly rough with goosebumps. I chose a seat at the table as far away from Greg as possible.

Bryan joined me. "You okay?" he murmured.

"Sure." I managed a smile. "Someone walking over my grave, I guess." Then I remembered thinking the same thing once before on this visit. When could it have been? Did it have something to do with Greg MacDonald? I couldn't remember. But one thing I *was* sure of was that Greg was not just an unpleasant man pretending to be a charmer. There was something basi-cally evil about him.

Don't be prejudiced! I told myself. After all I had absolutely nothing to go on but instinct. Yet I was ridiculously relieved when he left the table while we were still eating our lunch. I saw him a few minutes later walking down the steps towards the dock. Since he was wearing slacks and his navy blazer, he obviously wasn't going swimming. Glad though I was to see him go, I was suddenly curious about what he was up to.

Should I follow him? But then I'd be alone with him, and I certainly didn't want that.

Amanda was not so inhibited, however. As I struggled with mixed feelings of curiosity and caution, she jumped up and leaned over the railing. "Look. Where's Uncle Greg going, all dressed up like that?"

"What?" Bryan went to the railing. "I wonder if . . . ?" With his question unfinished he raced off the deck and pounded down the steps at a breakneck speed.

"Oh, do be careful!" Margaret exclaimed. "One of these days—"

"What a slime!" Amanda broke in.

"What is it? What's he doing?" I asked.

"Listen! You can hear the engine. He's gone off in *Moonlight*."

We hung over the deck railing until Bryan came into sight again, toiling up the path, his face red. His anger exploded as soon as he was within earshot. "You won't believe what Uncle Greg's done, Dad. He's taken *Moonlight* out without even asking. And we were planning to dive again this afternoon."

"That's too bad, Bry. But you can use the runabout, can't you?"

Bryan shook his head. "Our wetsuits and snorkelling gear are aboard, right there in plain sight. He must have done it deliberately. He *knew* we were going out again." He swallowed and took a deep breath. "Dad, you've got to stop him from interfering with our plans. He's *your* brother."

Was it my imagination, or did Bryan's father flinch at this last statement? But all he did was say mildly, "I'm sorry if Greg's upset your timetable, Bry, but there's not a lot I can do about it now that he's gone. Surely you youngsters can find something else to amuse yourselves with until he brings *Moonlight* back. After all, diving's not the be-all and end-all of your summer."

In the silence that followed this deflating remark, Margaret got to her feet. "If you're all through lunch, kids, perhaps you'd help me clear up. And if you're really at a loose end, I've got a grocery list as long as my arm."

"Okay, Mom. I can take a hint." Bryan sounded remarkably cheerful as he began to stack the plates, as if his anger had totally evaporated. When everything was cleared away and the few dishes were washed he looked at his mother's grocery list. "Wow, you weren't kidding, were you? I hope you can back this up with cash."

Margaret rummaged in her purse and handed over two fifty-dollar bills. "That should see you through."

"With enough left over for ice creams, pretty please?" Amanda put in.

"With my blessing. Now off you go. Don't be back too late. I do need some of that stuff for dinner tonight."

"Car keys?" Bryan held out his hand and she tossed him the keys.

"Dibs on the front seat," said Amanda quickly as we went out the front door to where all three cars were parked.

Bryan gave her a look and tilted his head towards the back of the Mercedes. "Guests get the front seat."

"Oh, all right. But you owe me." She slid obediently into the back of the car.

As we drove along the winding coastal road, flashing between tree shade and sun, I found myself watching Bryan. The farther we drove from the house, the farther away from the dive site, from the answer to the question that had haunted my family for years, the more frustrated I felt. I counted the wasted days. Five almost gone since the day I'd actually been introduced to Bryan. I took a deep breath and tried to imitate his laid-back attitude. In a very different way the dive was as important to him as it was to me, and yet he wasn't letting the delay get to him. *Here I am*, I told myself, *sitting next to a gorgeous hunk. So have fun*! And in a way I was. But even as I was aware of him sitting so close, of his eyes occasionally catching mine while he concentrated on the winding road, part of me couldn't let go of my mission. *These wasted days*.

"You're not mad at Greg any more. Why not?" I asked abruptly.

He glanced quickly at me and then back at the road. "Two reasons really," he said slowly. "The first is that I realized I didn't want Dad to know just how important this afternoon's dive would be."

"Why?"

"I don't want him to guess what we're doing—not till I've got the bell."

"Do you still think salvaging the bell is a good idea?"

"Sure I do. Face him with it and then he'll be able to put his bad memories aside—very psychological."

I chose my words carefully. "Have you ever thought that there might be something more to the wreck of *Far Skimmer*—more than just the memory of one terrifying day thirty years ago?"

Bryan drove on in silence. Obviously this possibility had never occurred to him. "You mean, something *more* than the storm?"

I bit my lip. *Should I tell him now? No, not yet. Maybe*

68

never. "I don't really know what I mean. But there are so many unanswered questions. For instance, why were they out in such a terrible storm in the first place?"

"I don't know whether Dad and Uncle Greg ever knew that. They were only kids, after all. Grandfather had all the answers. And he's gone."

"Maybe Gran knows something." Amanda spoke up from the back.

"She certainly put me in my place the only time I asked. But maybe she was only being grandmotherish."

"The needlepoint and playing bridge make you think that's all there is," Amanda explained. "You think there's nothing else. But underneath she's a very smart old lady. But I can't imagine Dad and Uncle Greg forgetting anything about that day, even if they were just kids. How could a person ever forget about nearly being drowned?"

"Your dad almost *did* forget, though, didn't he?" I looked over my shoulder at Amanda. "Didn't you live in the city and hardly ever come out to Treetops? Then for some reason you moved out here. You started hearing the bell. And everything became—difficult."

"Which doesn't make a lot of sense." Amanda scowled. "Anyway, what was the second reason you decided to be in a better temper, Bry?"

"Tell you when we've got the groceries. If what I suspect is right."

"No fair. I *hate* mysteries. I want to know *now*."

"Groceries first." He pulled into the supermarket parking lot and we pushed a cart through the aisles, hunting for the items on Margaret's list. It was fun, almost as if we were a real family shopping together. Bryan teased Amanda, sending her to hunt for imaginary and outrageous items, and she played along,

69

glowing in his attention. *How nice not to be an only kid*, I found myself thinking. Then, with a shock of reality that pulled me away from the warm family feeling, I remembered that Mom was an only too, but hadn't always been. Suddenly I felt outside, separate, watching Bryan and Amanda horse around as if I didn't know them at all.

The afternoon was half gone by the time we'd had got through the checkout and stowed the bags in the trunk of the car. "Time for ice cream. There's a place, Bry!"

"No, I want to try the one down by the marina." Bryan set off at a brisk pace and we almost had to run to catch up with him. But once he was on the boardwalk he slowed down, ignoring the cafe, and strolled along the edge of the wharves.

"*Bry!*" Amanda protested, but he walked on. "I hate it when he gets all mysterious," she muttered to me. "It's just a power thing, you know. What . . . ?"

He had come to a sudden halt. "Aha! As I suspected. Look." He strode rapidly along the last wharf, stopping at the very end. "There's the answer to your question, half-pint." He pointed.

"Why, it's *Moonlight*. What a nerve Uncle Greg has! Just bringing her out here and dumping her! I tell you what, Bry, let's take her back and leave him stranded. That'll show him."

"He'll have taken the key, you can bet on that. As I should have done. Stupid of me."

"Nonsense, Bryan," I protested. "You couldn't have expected your own uncle to make off with her. So what now?"

"I need to think. Let's get that ice cream."

"Right!" Amanda exclaimed joyfully and ran back to the boardwalk and along to the small cafe.

Bryan chose a table by the window with a view of the stretch of the marina where *Moonlight* was moored. "Sit tight and keep your eyes peeled, Amanda, in case he comes back."

"What'll you do if he does?"

"Probably murder him. But I don't think he'll appear. Your usual, sprout?"

"Yes, please."

I went to the counter with Bryan and helped him carry back the dishes of ice cream. Amanda dug silently into her concoction of rocky road and orange swirl, topped with whipped cream and sprinkles. As I spooned up my dish of caramel pecan I was once more conscious of Bryan sitting next to me, his arm close to mine. I was intensely aware of the hairs glistening gold against his tan, of two small moles, like a colon, on the back of his wrist.

"Penny for your thoughts?" he said suddenly and I blushed, pulling myself back to why we were here, eating ice cream at the marina.

"You don't expect him to take *Moonlight* back, do you?"

"Not really. I'd love to confront him, but I'm betting he's already gone." He shrugged.

"You think he's abandoned her and will just get a bus back when he's ready?"

"More likely a cab, knowing Uncle Greg. But yes. Now I've got to talk to the marina superintendent." He looked across the table at Amanda. "Eat up, pumpkin."

"I am, I am."

While we waited for Amanda to finish her dishful, we

sat silently listening to a love song coming softly over the local radio station. A sudden urgent voice broke into my sentimental thoughts. "The following is a weather advisory. A storm warning is in effect over the Great Lakes as an intense low pressure system moves eastward, bringing with it high winds and heavy precipitation. Gale-force winds are expected before morning."

"That's why he did it. He must have known." Bryan pushed his chair back and stood up, flushing angrily. "This afternoon was our last chance, maybe for days. But how did he know there was a storm warning?"

"Mom never has the radio on, but there *is* a portable in the guest room, Uncle Greg's room," Amanda pointed out.

"Our last chance for *days*?" I repeated in dismay.

"Quite likely. A really bad storm can last for quite a while. Man, he's been clever, planning to leave *Moonlight* here so we'd be stranded. Making it as difficult as possible for us to finish diving. If—"

"I know he's a slime, Bry. But why does he keep wanting to stop us?" Amanda interrupted.

"I don't know. But we certainly know he does. That's why he came as soon as he knew I'd finally found a diving buddy—to stop us if he could. Come on, let's go talk to Craig Millar. He's the marina supervisor, Sandra. He knows me. I often come here to get the tanks refilled. He'll tell us what Uncle Greg's up to."

"I warned him about the weather advisory," Craig told us. "That particular moorage is the most vulnerable in storms from the west. But he insisted it would be all right. He said he had to leave her for a couple of days. Something about waiting for a replacement part for the steering linkage . . ." He stopped and looked inquiringly at Bryan.

Bryan shook his head. "There's nothing whatever the matter with the steering—or with anything else on *Moonlight*. We were out in her all morning. She's running like a watch."

Craig shrugged. "Well, that's what he told me. I'm sorry. I know he's not the owner, but I took it for granted that he had the authority."

Bryan gave a humourless laugh. "Not only did he not ask us, he took off with all our diving gear aboard."

"That's too bad. Not that you'll be diving for a couple of days anyway. Maybe longer if this storm is as bad as they're predicting."

"I wish I could take her back this afternoon. The moorage at Treetops is a great deal more protected than the one here."

"Nothing to stop you, Bry. I insisted that he leave the key with me, though he didn't want to. I told him I had to have it in case I had to move her."

"Fantastic!"

Craig opened a file drawer and pulled out an envelope. He gave it a shake over the counter, and out fell the key and a piece of paper. He picked up the paper and slipped it back inside. "Our invoice. I'm afraid we can't return the deposit for the moorage."

Bryan laughed. "That's Uncle Greg's problem, not ours."

Craig peered out of the window. "Still clear out there, though the wind's beginning to get up. You should have a safe run back home." He handed over the key and showed Bryan where to sign in the marina logbook.

"I can't believe he did that!" Amanda burst out as we left the office. "Like I said, Uncle Greg's a slime!"

"Pipe down, half-pint. Sandra, I hope you have a valid driver's licence, or we've got a problem."

"You're in luck. I've got it here." I tapped my fanny pack. "Mom and Dad found it was convenient having a third driver for hauling antiques to the shop. But I hope Amanda plans to be my navigator rather than going with you. I'm not sure if I could find Treetops on my own."

Amanda was in top form as we drove along the winding road towards Treetops—towards home, I found myself thinking. In an unfamiliar and powerful car like the Mercedes I had to concentrate, and much of her chatter went in one ear and out the other. But she got my full attention a couple of times.

"Do you like Bry?"

"Why, yes, I guess so." I paused. "He's very nice," I finished lamely.

"Better than nice, *I* think."

Me too, I said to myself.

"Do you like living at Treetops?"

"It's wonderful. You're so lucky."

"We are, aren't we? When I'm at school I can't wait to get back, and I'm sorry for the kids who are stuck in the city all year round. Would you like to go on living here with us? I'd sure like it if you did."

I gave a forced laugh."It's not an option, Amanda."

"It *could* be," she said darkly.

I couldn't think of a thing to say. *What a kid!* I concentrated on the driving.

Safely home, we carried the bags of groceries into the kitchen. "Oh, good." Margaret looked up from her mixing bowl. "I need them right away. Why, where's Bryan?"

"Bringing Dad's property safely home. Mom, can you believe it? Uncle Greg took *Moonlight* into town and left her at the far end of the marina. With a storm coming up! And it wasn't by accident. He knew about the storm and Craig warned him about the moorage. You've got to talk to Dad about him. He's impossible."

Her mother sighed. "Amanda, you should know by now that I don't interfere between your dad and Greg. In-laws should stay out of family feuds. Now, where's the almond extract? I hope you remembered—"

"Here it is. Boy, that looks yummy."

"Fingers out! And they're not even clean. Really, Amanda! You may lick the bowl when I'm through and not before."

"Don't forget." Amanda leaned on the counter and stared at her mother. "Mom, does Dad ever talk to you about *Far Skimmer*?"

"What?" Margaret turned suddenly and her beater splashed the counter. "Now look what you've made me do. Be dears, both of you, and put away the groceries for me. Then get out of my kitchen. You're distracting me."

As we went downstairs afterwards Amanda said, "Let's go talk to Gran about Greg."

"No!" I almost shouted and then tried to cover up. "I mean, I don't think that's a great idea, Amanda. Bryan did tell us he wanted to keep what we're doing a secret until . . . until he's salvaged the bell. If we suddenly start asking questions about *Far Skimmer*, people are going to suspect us of something."

"Sorry. I forgot. Say, let's be useful and go down to

the dock. We ought to make sure the runabout's tied up snugly before the storm. And Bryan should be along pretty soon anyway."

We had just secured the small boat with extra buffers between her hull and the side of the dock when the sound of *Moonlight*'s engine made us both look up. "That's good," Amanda said. "I was afraid the storm would reach us before he got back."

"Really?" I looked up at the sun. "It still looks great out there."

"See those clouds in the southwest? And the wind's blowing a lot harder. It'll be here soon, you'll see."

I smiled to myself at Amanda's sudden air of wisdom. She often acted a lot older than almost twelve. Probably the result of hanging out with grown-ups and a brother five years older. But then she'd suddenly revert to being a little kid—like when she told me I could stay with them at Treetops forever. *Dream on, Sandra*, I mocked myself.

I looked across the water, past the small islands on whose shores the water was already beginning to break in white spray, to the place where we planned to dive. Would it be tomorrow? Or would we have to wait till the next day? Or even the day after? That didn't bear thinking about. I bit my lip and then tried to smile as Bryan steered *Moonlight* towards the shore.

"Glad you're here," he shouted as he slid the launch neatly up to the dock and cut the engine. "We'll have to tie her down really well. It's going to be quite a blow."

"Even in this sheltered cove?" I looked around at the calm anchorage.

"Even here. When the wind's in this quarter the waves can really build up with nothing in their way to slow

76

then down. I just hope it's not bad enough to shift *Far Skimmer* again."

"Do you want us to take in the wetsuits and snorkels, Bry?"

"Sure, sprout. Dump them on the dock and we'll rinse them out and hang them up once we've got everything shipshape here."

"And don't forget the key!"

"You bet I won't." He showed us that he already had it hanging around his neck on a piece of string.

By the time *Moonlight* was safely secured and we had rinsed off our wetsuits and hung them up in the boathouse, the day was darkening ominously. The wind lashed the trees as we climbed the steps to the house, and the first coin-sized drops fell as we ran inside.

"Bry, will you put away the deck furniture?" Margaret called from the kitchen, and we hurried out again to fold up the chairs and tables and store them in the cabinet built against the far end of the deck. It was raining seriously as we ran in, shaking ourselves dry. Bryan secured the doors and windows. "It's sure turning cold!"

"Why don't you start a fire?" Margaret suggested. "And my mixing bowl's ready for anyone who wants to lick it."

"Me, me! Bry can light the fire." Amanda made for the kitchen.

I crouched down on the hearth rug and watched the flames lick upwards as Bryan added kindling and then split logs to the crumpled newspaper in the grate. We both jumped when Greg spoke behind us. "Have you kids been here all afternoon?"

Bryan turned from the fire to stare at his uncle, and I could see the muscle at the corner of his jaw jump. "No.

We went into town to get groceries. How about you?"

"I just went for a spin. Hope I didn't spoil your fun taking *Moonlight*."

"Not a bit, thank you, Uncle Greg. And you don't have to worry about her. We found her at the marina and brought her safely back."

I saw Greg flush. His lips tightened. "That was a mistake, Bryan. Her engine sounded a bit rough so I left her at the marina for an inspection."

"Oh? That's funny. Craig said you told *him* the problem was in the steering. You'd better get your story straight before you explain to Dad why you took *Moonlight* without asking, with all our gear aboard, and then left her in that bad moorage when you knew a severe storm was coming."

Greg gave an uneasy laugh. "How you kids do exaggerate. This storm'll be just a bit of a blow, you'll see. The boat would have come to no harm." He went into the kitchen where we could hear him talking to Margaret.

Amanda came out, an expression of disgust on her face. "*Slime!*" she whispered.

"Amanda, wash your sticky fingers at once," her mother called. Amanda groaned, but obediently went into the powder room off the front hall. When she came back she squatted by the fire, warming her hands. "He was asking me exactly what Craig said to you. Don't worry. I didn't tell him anything."

"I think he's getting panicky," I whispered. "And that's making him reckless—and stupid. We must be extra careful."

Bryan nodded, put his finger to his lips and got to his feet. "The fire's fine now," he said in a cheerful, over-loud voice. "Let's do a jigsaw puzzle while the storm's here. There's a new three-thousand piece one I've been wanting to do. I hope you're good at jigsaws, Sandra."

How appropriate, I thought as Bryan spilled the pieces onto the table by the window. *Putting pieces together to try to make sense of the whole picture.*

The next three days were weird. Some hours seemed to stretch out forever, hours punctuated by the splendid meals Margaret whipped up, hours in which I could see our opportunity for the final necessary dive vanishing in the storm. But at other times, when the three of us worked on the jigsaw, or sat cosily by the fire toasting muffins or marshmallows and talking in the casual, relaxed way of people getting to know each other really well, the hours flew by. I was comfortable at Treetops. Only once in a while did a sobering thought jolt me back to reality. *The life of the rich and famous, Sandra. Better not get used to it. Because if you're right, it won't be yours for much longer.*

In keeping with this depressing idea was the behaviour of Don MacDonald. He did not appear at the table for any of Margaret's great meals, but occasionally took a tray of food back to his office and emerged at intervals to refill his coffee mug. By the second day of the storm he was not even bothering to get dressed, but shuffling out in his dressing gown, unshaven and red-eyed, his hands shaking.

"You're drinking far too much coffee, Don," Margaret exclaimed. "And not eating enough. What can I get for you? There must be something you'd like."

"Just peace and quiet," he snapped back and retreated to his office. The sound of Wagner's "Ride of the Valkyrie" roared out at us as he opened the door.

Margaret put her hands over her ears. "Peace and quiet?" she repeated to the closed door, and I saw her eyes fill with tears. I turned away, pretending not to notice, and called Amanda to help with the puzzle.

In contrast Greg seemed to thrive on the noise of the storm and the thundering of Wagner, and on the almost electrical tension in the house. When the storm was at its most vicious, lashing boughs against the roof, he stood looking at the rain streaming down the window panes, chuckling to himself.

"What's so funny?" Amanda muttered under her breath, and Bryan gave her a warning frown. Luckily Greg didn't seem to hear, and we ignored him as he strolled by the table where we were working. The big puzzle was more than half finished. We'd established the framework of straight-edged pieces and had been busily working inwards, piece by piece, but even with three of us at it, there was still a large blank space in the middle.

"What can the picture be?" I asked in frustration. "The leftover pieces don't give us much of a clue."

"Please let us look at the cover of the box, Bry," Amanda pleaded. "Just one little peek?"

"Nope. You know perfectly well that it's a house rule. And no sneaking."

In fact he had put the box away in the closet as soon as he had tipped out the pieces three days before. All I could make out, as I looked at the half-finished jigsaw, was that it was a rendition of a medieval painting, a busy village scene with countryside in the background. But was that the tip of a church spire? I wondered. And the piece in my hand, was it part of a five-barred gate— or maybe the entrance to a jail? It was all so ambiguous.

Like Amanda, I longed for a look at the picture on the box to make sense of what remained to be done.

It's like the search for Far Skimmer, *I thought. Will I find what Mom and Dad expect? Or do all the little clues—the puzzle pieces—amount to something quite innocent and very different from the terrible conclusion they have reached? If only the storm would end so I could find out for sure.*

"If only the storm would stop," Amanda sighed, echoing my thoughts. "It usually doesn't last for more than a couple of days, does it, Bry?"

"Don't fuss, sprout. It'll be over when it's over." He stretched and looked out the window. "But I do believe it's a bit lighter over there."

"Tomorrow," breathed Amanda. "Yay!"

"Don't forget that we'll have to wait for the water to clear before we do any more diving," he said firmly. "Come on. Keep your mind on the puzzle."

Privately, when we were alone without Greg's skulking presence, Bryan said to me, "I'm sorry the storm's wasted so much of your holiday. I realize it's been eight days since we met, and we've only just confirmed where *Far Skimmer* is. How long *can* you stay?"

I shrugged, as if it weren't the most important thing in my life. "We only had two weeks of holidays altogether, so Mom and Dad will need to pick me up in two days max. How soon do you think we'll be able to go down?"

"It really is clearing. Maybe we'll get a chance to dive tomorrow afternoon—if we're lucky."

I bit my lip. *I can't leave without finding out. Not after we've waited so long and planned it so carefully. I can't.*

81

chapter FIVE

ON WHAT I now thought of, rather desperately, as Day Nine, I woke early with a shaft of brilliant sunshine in my eyes. I sat up, blinking. No sound of wind or driving rain. I pulled open the drape across the French window. As the light flooded in Amanda sat up, her hair standing on end like a rooster's on top of her head.

"Sunshine!" she exclaimed and ran out of the room. I could hear her shrill voice and Bryan's deeper one reply from the room next door.

"We're to check the gear and get it aboard *Moonlight* right after breakfast," she reported back to me. "Your first scuba diving day!"

About time, I thought. I knew I should feel relieved, but I had an edgy feeling as if my careful plans, which had fallen into place so smoothly when Bryan first asked me to dive with him, were slowly turning sour.

"What about your uncle Greg?" I asked as the three of us walked down the path after breakfast.

"Well, I've hung onto the key to *Moonlight*, so he can't pull that trick again," Bryan said cheerfully.

"You know him better than I do," I answered, speaking carefully. "But don't you think it's possible that he might try to interfere again—maybe by putting your gear out of action?"

"That's true, Bry. He could have done something already because our stuff's been sitting in the boathouse all this time," Amanda said excitedly. "He's such a slime!"

"Take it easy, sprout. He couldn't have gone down during the storm without our noticing—he'd have come back soaked. But we *will* be extra careful checking everything out. And we'll make sure not to leave our gear alone—you're right, Sandra. We'll take no chances. One of us will need to stay on guard all the time."

I was impressed with the care Bryan took inspecting our equipment, even sampling the air in each of the tanks.

"No carbon monoxide," he said when Amanda asked what he was doing. "It *can* happen if the compressed air is contaminated by the exhaust from a nearby engine. But there'll be no accidents today."

We decided to take it in turns to go up for lunch, and it was while I was alone on the dock that Greg came strolling down the steps towards the lake. I tried to ignore him, but he came over and stood next to me, uncomfortably close. I moved away.

"So, Cassandra, do you have any dire prophecies for us today?"

I managed a smile. "Why do you ask? Are you expecting trouble? Or maybe just causing it?"

"Me? Trouble is *your* first name, not mine."

"So why are you here?" I challenged him.

"In general, as to my life? Or, more particularly, at Treetops? Or, specifically, down at the dock talking to you? I'll answer the last question—the rest is my business. Bry says for you to go up to the house for your lunch."

Nice try, I thought. "No, thanks. I'm not that hungry. I'll wait till they get back."

"I can't persuade you? No? Very well. I'm not one for diving myself, but I think I'll come along for the ride this afternoon. A spot of fresh air and sunshine on the water, you know, a change after having been cooped up in the house for so long, listening to brother Don's interminable Wagner."

"I guess you'll have to ask Bryan about that."

"'Have to ask Bryan,'" he mimicked. "Maybe I will, Cassandra. Maybe I will." And with that he strolled back up to the house while I watched him anxiously and willed Bryan and Amanda to come down quickly so we could get away.

"Let's go out now," I begged as soon as they appeared.

"But you haven't had anything to eat."

"I don't care. Let's just get going before he comes back."

"Okay." Bryan nodded. "No panic, Sandra. We've got everything we need on board."

As soon as we boarded *Moonlight* Bryan started the engine and slowly backed the launch away from the dock. A chuckle from Amanda brought me to the railing. Greg was running down the steps to the dock. "Wait," he called over the water. "Phone call for Cassandra. From her parents."

Bryan slowed down. "Want to go back?"

"Of course not. It's just a ploy. They're not checking up on me. Keep going."

Amanda waved at Greg, who was dancing with rage on the end of the dock. *Greg knows the truth*, I thought. *He doesn't want us to find* Far Skimmer. We watched him stamp up the steps to the house as Bryan guided *Moonlight* out to the dive site. There was still a swell, a memory of the storm, but Bryan said cheerfully that it wasn't enough to be a problem. "The water's going to be a bit murky, but now that we know where we're going

84

that shouldn't be a real problem. With dive lights we'll be okay." He cut the engine and dropped the anchor.

"Sure this is the right place?" His navigation still amazed me. Islands. Rocks. Trees. One bit looking much like the next.

"Trust me. I had a good look around after our last dive. See that tall jack pine on the rock over there? It's in line with the microwave tower on the north shore. And that buoy over to the east is just a smidgen to the right of the fixed light at the end of the big island. See?"

I stared at the two sets of reference points, trying to fix them in my mind for later, in case I should need them. *Jack pine to the microwave tower: one line. Buoy to the fixed light: the second line. X marks the spot.*

"But you don't have to worry about that," Bryan went on, noticing my concentration. "After all, I'm the designated navigator."

"Sure." I gave him what I hoped was a reassuring smile, though my face felt tense. Finally the moment I'd been waiting for was close, unbearably close. What would I find?

Bryan and I struggled into our wetsuits, helping each other with buoyancy vests and tanks, attaching our weight belts and all the additional paraphernalia. We looked over each other's system, checking each item aloud, while Amanda watched enviously. Depth gauge and watch, dive compass and knife, light, underwater slate for necessary comments or instructions.

"Everything okay," Bryan said at last. "Put out the dive flag, Amanda, and be prepared to repel boarders."

I stared. "You're joking, aren't you?" I asked uncertainly.

"Of course. Amanda knows that, don't you, sprout?"

"But you will be careful, won't you, Bry?" Amanda's voice was shrill, and I was sure that it hadn't seemed like a joke to her either. The kid was no fool.

One by one we stepped off the launch and prepared to begin our descent. Bryan had judged his markers perfectly. As I looked down I could see *Far Skimmer* directly below us, looming out of the murk, a slender shadow like a huge basking shark. She had listed slightly since the storm, settling on the landward side of the reef, so that her deck was at about a sixty-degree angle to the lake floor.

We adjusted our buoyancy, hovering amidships above the slanted deck. Bryan jerked his thumb aft, and I nodded and gestured that I was going to look around while he unshipped the bell.

I waited till Bryan had turned away and then swam towards the companionway, which had obviously been closed off during the storm. That was no surprise to me. I examined the entrance and found that it was, in fact, in two parts: a hatch that slid open to give headroom, and a small door off the lower deck that fitted snugly into the frame and against the closed hatch. Dad had explained to me what I might find.

I had little hope of sliding open the hatch after all these years of the wood swelling in the water. Instead I concentrated on the door. I braced myself with one hand against the frame and pulled on the latch with the other. It didn't budge. Swollen by years underwater, I realized. Or perhaps jammed by the movement of the ship on the reef. *I'll need something to force it—find a crowbar or something*, I told myself. I wasted no more time, but swam around to the side, where I knew the saloon windows would be.

I moved cautiously, trying not to stir up the silt that coated the deck. I hovered by the saloon windows, four small squares. I peered in, my mask close against the glass. Nothing but darkness.

I detached my dive lamp from my belt and shone it through the glass. At first it only reflected my own face—bug-eyes, mouth distorted by the regulator—looking like an alien. But when I held the lamp close to the glass and pressed my face alongside it, careful not to dislodge my mask, I caught glimpses of the room within. Small glimpses, like the separate pieces of a jigsaw . . .

Narrow beams of light from my dive lamp touched a cupboard door sagging ajar, its contents strewn on the floor. Then a couch, the upholstery of which had been transformed by the years into a uniform grey-green velvet. A can must have rolled across the floor during the recent storm, leaving a small trail behind it, like a miniature bulldozer. I found myself wondering how long it would take for the silt to settle once more and cover up that narrow line.

As my light wavered along the floor, it picked up a litter of cans, their labels soaked off, rusted to copper brown. There was a broken platter and a mug, miraculously whole, sitting upright on the velvety silted carpet. Then something that was neither can nor crockery, almost out of sight.

My heart gave a huge thump, and I was suddenly dizzy and disoriented. I reeled back against the guard rail, feeling myself spinning away into nothingness. I forced myself to take a deep, calming breath and check my displays. Time elapsed, okay. Air supply, okay. I took another breath and, once more in control, pushed off from the rail to the next window and shone my light downward.

There, on the floor of the saloon, was the evidence I needed—the evidence I was beginning to hope I wouldn't find. I had come to the end of the search that had begun so long ago. A search that had been taken up by Dad when Mom had first told him the sad story, the story that ended only with a question. A search that *I* in turn had taken up; like a baton in a relay race, the need to know the truth had been passed from one to the other.

What had caught my eye—the different shape—looked at first glance like a slender cardboard tube dusted over with silt. But cardboard would have disintegrated long ago. Bones did not. Bones remained. *Remains.*

They seemed so small, so fragile, these bones. What I had expected? Thirty years ago he had been only eight years old, four years younger than Greg, five years younger than Don MacDonald. Only a child, eager for adventure, easily lured aboard *Far Skimmer* on what was to be her last voyage—and his.

How had it happened? How had the boys managed to smuggle him aboard and hide him in the cabin without their father knowing? Why had he stayed below while Greg and Don were on deck with their dad? Why had they not remembered him when the storm struck, when their father decided to head across the lake to the safety of their home anchorage rather than turn back? Why had they done nothing to rescue him when *Far Skimmer* struck the reef? Could they have actually *forgotten* him? That was the saddest possibility of all.

The water wouldn't have filled the cabin at once. It

first had to displace the air inside, and that would have taken time. Time enough for the child to wade through the rising water and climb the stairs and push the door open. To *try* to push the door open. Had it stuck then too?

I remembered reading the report that Don and Greg's father had given the provincial police, how they had escaped the foundering yacht in the dinghy, lucky to be wearing life jackets. How they had struggled to free themselves from the grasp of the hungry water trying to pull them down after the sinking yacht, how they had had to bail for their lives as they made for shore. It must have been a desperate time. Easy enough to forget their passenger. But afterwards: *To say nothing. Ever. But to remember, always . . . every time a storm set the ship's bell tolling for the dead, for the forgotten.*

A hand tapped my shoulder and I jumped, the dive lamp slipping from my fingers and twirling at the end of its cord. But of course it was only Bryan, tapping his watch, jabbing his thumb upward. *Time? It can't be time already.*

I backed away from the window. *But I won't forget you,* I promised silently. *I will return.*

We ascended slowly, side by side, the anchor rope our guideline to the world above. When we stopped at the fifteen-foot level I stared at him. *How blank his face is, behind the mask. I have no idea what he's thinking. Just as well. If he could read my thoughts*—I reminded myself to get under control before surfacing and unmasking. I looked away from him, down into the receding depths. Beside the anchor rope a twin cord snaked down. At the end of it must be the bell. I glanced quickly back at Bryan and he made a circle sign—A-OK—with finger and thumb. It was time to rise to the surface, to feel the waves against my face, drops beading my mask. And there was Amanda, hanging over the railing, her face eager and anxious. She grabbed the line from Bryan and fastened it off to the railing before taking our weight belts and helping us aboard.

"Bryan, you got it! You've done it! But do you want *him* to know?"

"Uncle Greg? No. Not yet. Not till I'm ready to announce my find."

"He's probably watching us. Lurking behind the islands, I expect." Her voice was shaky. "He came out in the runabout right after you went down. He was horrid. He kept circling around, like a . . . like a shark. And I screamed at him to keep his distance. 'It's the law when we're flying the dive flag!' I yelled, but he didn't listen. He wouldn't leave till I threatened to call the police on the radio. Then he moved off." She was almost in tears and Bryan gave her a wet hug.

"Good girl. You did great. Not to worry. We'll pull the bell up—lucky it's on the far side from land—and then we'll hide it in one of the bags with our diving gear."

While he hauled up his trophy, Amanda and I stood shoulder to shoulder, facing the land, pointing and talking as if we were not in the least interested in what Bryan was up to behind us. My thoughts were racing. *Greg knows, that's certain. He's frantic to stop our dives. But what about the others—Don MacDonald? Margaret? And the senior Mrs. MacDonald? Are they all in on the secret?*

I shivered, realizing that I hated even Amanda and Bryan as part of this family, tainted with the same

90

money and power. Yet I could still feel myself attracted to Bryan. *How did I get into this mess?* I thought.

I jumped as he spoke just behind me. "I'll take the bell below," he said. "Let's put him off by staying out for a while longer. Could you heat up some chocolate in the galley, Amanda, while we get out of our wetsuits?"

Alone on deck I shivered. Just cold, I told myself, peeling off my wetsuit and wrapping a towel round me. I tried to push the image of the scatter of small bones out of my mind. As soon as Bryan came up in jeans and a heavy Aran sweater, I went below and pulled on heavy wool pants and a turtleneck over my swimsuit.

Amanda called up to Bryan. "The chocolate's hot!"

"No sign of the runabout," he reported as he clattered down the companionway.

"Where's the bell?" Her voice was shrill with excitement.

"In my bag." He reached for it. "Ta-dah!"

"Oh." Amanda's face fell. "I thought it would be shiny."

"It's not gold, sprout. It's brass. Don't worry. Before we present it to Dad I aim to clean it up. It'll be as shiny as new."

"Look, here's the name engraved on the side." Amanda ran her finger over it. *"Far Skimmer.* Grandfather must have had that done years and years ago. Imagine, all that time under the lake, long before we were born. Isn't it amazing?"

I stared, unseeing, at the tarnished bell. As far as Bryan was concerned, our mission was over. But for me the worst was still to come. "When do you plan to make the presentation?" I asked casually.

"Later today, I guess. I hadn't got that far in my planning."

"We should make a big deal over it." Amanda's voice went up excitedly. "Like, present it when everyone's together during dinner. You make an announcement, Bry, and I'll carry the bell in sitting on a cushion. What do you think?"

"I think you'll look pretty silly making an entrance sitting on a cushion, sprout."

"Bry! The *bell* on a cushion—like a crown, you know."

Their voices—Amanda's shrill with eagerness, Bryan's deep, but with an undercurrent of excitement in it too—hardly penetrated the thoughts that whirled around in my head. *All this play-acting. It seems so trivial. How will they react when I tell them my story—the real story? If I do. Maybe I should just leave them to their triumph.* I told myself that I'd answered Mom's question. I knew what had happened, and now our family had some kind of closure. Was that enough? No, not really. I still needed the final proof. But how was I going to get it if the presentation was planned for after dinner this very day? That didn't leave me much time.

"Sandra?" Bryan's voice brought me back to the moment. "Sandra, you're miles away. What do you think?"

"Huh? Well, it's *your* family, Bryan . . . What you decide to do isn't really my business." I stumbled over my words.

"Come on! Without your help I couldn't have dived. I couldn't have found *Far Skimmer*. Of course you're involved too."

"Anyway, you're our friend. Go ahead, Sandra, tell us what you think."

Our friend. Amanda's innocent words were like a knife jab. I almost winced. What I had to tell them would destroy their triumph, and I would be exposed as the spy I was. We could never be friends again after that. For an instant I was tempted to forget it. To let them enjoy their great surprise. Then leave, my secret intact. But I couldn't, could I? Greg knew. I was certain of that.

I spoke cautiously. "I wonder if such a public presentation might not be a bit—a bit overwhelming. For your father, I mean. And Greg too, of course."

"Slimy Uncle Greg! I can't wait to see his face when we show them the bell. He's been against us since the beginning. He's the enemy."

"Why?"

"What do you mean, Sandra? It's obvious. He never wanted us to find *Far Skimmer*."

"I know that, Amanda. I meant—well, have either of you ever thought about *why* Greg didn't want you to find the yacht?"

"Not really," Bryan said slowly. "It's just been a given, ever since I first brought up the idea of diving around here instead of going across the lake to the regular wreck sites. It was Uncle Greg who reminded Dad that I couldn't dive on my own. Then when Amanda said you were coming—"

"You know what I think?" Amanda interrupted eagerly. "I think he really enjoys seeing Dad upset whenever there's a storm. Now that Bry's got the bell Uncle Greg won't be able to do that any more."

"Hmm. What do you think, Sandra? You still don't look satisfied."

"For a start, how did Greg know you were after the bell? That's always been a secret, hasn't it?"

"You mean there's another reason why he didn't want me to find *Far Skimmer*? You've got an idea about that, haven't you?"

I shook my head. "Maybe I'll tell you later. I'm not sure. There's something I've still got to work out. Forget about it."

Bryan gave me a penetrating look that made me deeply uneasy. I told myself that he couldn't guess—not possibly. I sat silently until he shrugged. "Okay. Let's go ashore and get the bell polished up for this evening's performance."

After we arrived back at the house Amanda got a can of brass polish and some rags from her mother, and we went down to Bryan's room. The door was shut and when Bryan opened it, we saw that he had drawn the curtains across the windows. "So no one will spoil the surprise."

"Like Uncle Greg!"

I had made up my mind about what I had to do. And it had to be now. "Look, it only takes one person to polish a bell. Bryan, may I borrow Amanda for an hour? Something I have to finish."

"Sure. I'll have this shined up by the time you get back." He patted the bell in a proprietary manner as we left him to it. I was thankful that his preoccupation stopped him from asking me what I was up to.

"What is it, Sandra? You look awfully mysterious," Amanda whispered.

"Come outside. Where no one can overhear us."

"Okay!" Amanda skipped out of the house and we went down the steps towards the dock. "So what's the secret?"

"I've got to go out to the wreck one more time and I'll need your help."

Amanda's face fell. "I'm not allowed to take *Moonlight* out on my own."

"Oh. The runabout then. Can you handle that?"

"Of course. But why? Sandra, you're not planning another *dive*, are you? Without Bry? You mustn't. Not alone."

"I have to. Please trust me, Amanda. I won't be long. There's just one thing I have to—to verify."

Amanda frowned. "I don't understand. Why didn't you do whatever it was you needed to do when you were down with Bryan?"

"I couldn't. There wasn't time."

"Suppose there's an accident? Suppose you're trapped down there? You could *drown*. What would I do?"

"It's not going to happen. Please, Amanda. It's terribly important. It's—it's the real reason I'm here."

Amanda stared. "I don't know what you mean. Bryan picked *you* as a diving buddy."

I shook my head. "No. I picked *him*. So I could dive at this site. So I could find out the truth. 'And the truth shall make you free,'" I found myself quoting.

"What truth?" Amanda's eyes widened and I could see tears glistening, unshed. She no longer looked eleven going on twelve, but like a disappointed little girl. "What do you mean? You don't sound like our friend any more. You sound like—like a spy."

"In a way I suppose I am. But that doesn't stop me from wanting to go on being your friend. And Bryan's too, I hope. Please, Amanda, don't make an issue of it. Let's just *go*."

"Why won't you let Bryan help you? If it's that important, you can tell him whatever it is you've got to do."

I shook my head and stripped off my pants and heavy sweater.

"You've been planning this all along, haven't you? How do you know I'll help you?" Amanda accused me.

"I don't. But I'll go out on my own if I have to." I pulled on my wetsuit, put a new cylinder into the buoyancy vest and, with Amanda's reluctant help, put it on and adjusted it. Weights. Light. "Now all I need is some sort of pry bar. Have you got anything among those tools over there?"

"Like this?" Amanda lifted a crowbar from the shelf at the back of the boathouse.

"Perfect." I fastened it by a length of cord to my belt.

"But what's it *for*? What are you going to *do*?"

I ignored her questions. "Got my fins? Thanks. You *are* coming, aren't you? *Please*."

She hung back. "It's not right. Let me get Bry. You know he'd be glad to help."

"Uh-uh. The two of us can handle this. Think of it as our special adventure. Yours and mine." Her expression changed, caution giving way to excitement.

"An adventure? Oh, but we shouldn't."

"Come on, sprout. Nothing venture, nothing win." I walked briskly down the dock to where the small runabout was moored across from *Moonlight*.

Amanda followed slowly, unhitched the boat from its mooring and climbed aboard, holding the rope with a single turn about its post. The engine started easily, and with a gentle purr the runabout nudged away from the dock.

"Haul in the rope, Sandra. And you've going to have

to tell me when we're there. Do you remember Bry's directions?"

"Oh, yes. I remember."

We were almost out of sight when a faint shout from the direction of the stairs made us look back.

"It's Bry. He's going to be awfully mad, Sandra."

"He'll understand once it's over—anyway, I hope he will. Don't worry about him now. Just carry on the way you're going, Amanda. Okay, slow down. A bit to the right. Yes, that's it. Anchor us here."

"How long will you be?"

"Maybe fifteen minutes."

"I wish you wouldn't. It's not safe. *Never* dive without a buddy. That's the rule."

"I have to, Amanda." I wriggled into my fins, adjusted my mask and mouthpiece and, hand over mask, somersaulted into the water.

Beneath the surface the sun still shone through the riffling waves in patterns of light and dark. I could feel my heart thudding against my chest wall, my breathing harsh through my regulator. I forced myself to be calm, to breathe slowly, gently. Guided by the anchor rope I swam down into stillness, into the dim light and cold water of the lake.

I had remembered the spot perfectly. The anchor rope hung almost straight down beside me. Ahead, no more than a dozen strokes away, lay the dark bulk of *Far Skimmer*. Had it tilted even more? The deck seemed to be almost forty-five degrees off the level. Suppose it were to turn turtle?

I pushed the gruesome thought away and gently kicked my way along the sloping deck until I reached the door at the top of the companionway, the door that

led down to the main cabin. I tugged at the handle
again but, as before, the door refused to budge. Wood
swollen with years of immersion in the water had made
an almost impenetrable seal.

*What if I can't break in? What if? No. That can't
happen. Everything has gone just as we planned. It can't
fall apart now. I've got to get in. I've got to get the proof
myself.*

I forced the toothed end of the crowbar against the
frame, but as soon as I tried to lean against the bar, I
just spun away. The problem was the lack of gravity.
Balanced as I was in the almost weightless condition of
underwater, I could exert little force.

"Give me where to stand, and I will move the earth,"
some ancient Greek was supposed to have said. I only
wanted to move one little door, not the world, but without a solid place to stand—a fulcrum—it was impossible. *Fifteen minutes max*, I had promised Amanda. How
much of that allotted time had I already wasted?

I wrapped my legs around the railing—not easy to do
with flippers attached—and again pushed against the
frame. Something gave. I tightened my hold and tried
again. My legs were beginning to cramp and I knew I
couldn't keep this up much longer. One more try. I took
a deep breath, knowing that I was using up my air at an
alarming rate with this extra exertion, and pushed.

The crowbar flipped out of my hands and spun away,
twisting at the end of its restraining cord. But I didn't
need it any more. My fingers, clumsy with cold, jerked
at the door and it opened slowly against the pressure of
the surrounding water.

I shone my flashlight down the slanted tunnel of the
companionway and flutter-kicked slowly downward,

arms stretched ahead of me, the light in my left hand. Soft greyness lay like a pall over every surface. Careful not to cloud the visibility by touching anything, I moved slowly forward.

The table took up much of the saloon, with couches on either side built against the walls and cupboards above and below. Rusty cans lay in heaps on the seats; others had rolled to the floor. I swept my flashlight across the carpet, illuminating patch after patch, until it caught a gleam of white.

I could hear my blood pounding in my ears, the sound of my harsh breathing. There it was, what I had been searching for, but had dreaded finding. Scattered by the lurches of the ship as she had settled over the years was the sad evidence. The once white bones, now covered with silt, the shreds of clothing, remains of a cotton shirt and shorts, still holding together the main bones of spine, pelvis and shoulder blades. His sandals must have drifted away, long separated from the feet that had worn them. At first I could see no head. Then, as my lamp wavered across the floor, the skull jumped suddenly into focus over in a corner, quite apart from the body.

In spite of knowing that it would be there, of steeling myself to accept that inevitability, I couldn't stop a great convulsive shudder. The light wavered crazily around the room. I wanted to open my mouth and let out a great scream. My jaw muscles clenched on the rubber of my mouthpiece.

I needed one last piece of evidence. If the skeleton had been intact it would have been around the neck, but now I realized I would have to search for it, wasting more precious time. I glanced at my watch and quickly looked away again. *That much time used up already?*

99

I steadied the flashlight and began a systematic search along the angle where the tilting floor met the couch. I couldn't leave without this final missing piece. Once it was in my hand, the last two years of planning, of learning how to dive, of investigating the lives and movements of the MacDonald family and being accepted into their midst—all this would be over. I could go home.

I hovered just above the floor, the fingers of my right hand gently feeling along the angle between floor and couch. Once something grabbed me and held me back. Panic surged through me. *Steady*, I told myself. *The hose is caught on something, that's all.* I backed slowly away until I was free, moved closer to the floor and went on searching. If only my hands weren't so cold. I could hardly feel anything.

I had almost given up when my outstretched fingers touched something small and hard. I managed to grab it and bring it close to my mask. I'd been looking for something that shone in the flashlight, but of course it didn't. I should have remembered that from seeing the bell. It was as black as if it had been painted, a thin chain, still fastened, with a medal dangling from it.

With it twined in my fingers I backed up and turned carefully to face the companionway. There was a creak, enormously loud underwater, and *Far Skimmer* shuddered as if she were alive. What was happening? My nightmare of being trapped seemed in danger of coming true.

As fast as I dared I flutter-kicked up the companionway. Why was it so dark? I shone my light ahead of me and the reflection bounced back off the wooden surface of the door. It had swung shut. That was all, I told

myself. Just a push and I would be free. I pushed. I
turned the handle and pushed again. All around me,
over the sound of my breathing and heartbeat, was a
steady, ominous creaking. *Far Skimmer* was sliding
farther down the reef, and the door frame twisting out
of true.

I became aware of the chain still clutched in my right
hand. I'd need both hands to get out of this death trap.
Would two hands be enough? Carefully I tucked the
precious relic into a pocket on my buoyancy control
vest and fastened the pocket down. It would be unthink-
able to come so far and lose what I'd come for.

Again I glanced quickly at my watch and swallowed.
Amanda must be going crazy with worry. I had been
down here far longer than I'd planned. I looked at my
tank capacity indicator, almost afraid of what I would
see. Close to the red. Five hundred pounds was the cut-
off pressure, the amount of air that would allow me to
reach the surface safely. I twisted the door handle
again, put my shoulder to the wood, kicking hard
behind me. Clouds of silt rose around me. Nothing
budged. I was trapped.

I could feel my eyes darken. There was a roaring in
my ears, as if I were about to faint. *It can't be the air. I
just checked it. Only panic. Stop it, Sandra!*

I forced myself to breathe slowly, evenly. It was going
to be all right. It had to be all right. I had come so far.

Gradually my panic subsided. There was a banister
on the right side of the companionway. With the ship
tilted the way it was, this was now almost overhead. I
grabbed it with both hands, brought my feet up so that
my fins were flat against the door and pushed.

My feet flew away over my head and I found myself

somersaulting backward. The crowbar came up and banged against my face mask. I grabbed it, suddenly remembering that first dive when Bryan had flipped the mask from my face to test my behaviour under stress.

I'd passed that test easily. This was quite another challenge. I pushed the crowbar into the crack in the door and managed to wedge it there. I tucked my knees against my chest and pushed with my feet against the door once more. This time I didn't slip, but the door still wouldn't budge.

Water's not compressible the way air is, I reminded myself. This wasn't like opening a door on dry land. At this depth the weight of water on either side was keeping the door firmly in place. That must be the problem. It couldn't really be jammed again. I told myself that all I had to do was to keep pushing until the door gave way. Or till I ran out of air.

How had Christopher felt, waking up in the cabin to find the water rising slowly towards the ceiling? Hearing the wind, feeling the shudder of the ship as *Far Skimmer* pounded against the waves? Had he climbed up the companionway and pounded his fists on the door, yelling for them to let him out, trying desperately to make his small voice heard over the screaming of the storm?

At least I haven't been forgotten, I thought bleakly. *Amanda knows where I am. She can get Bryan to help. But by then it will be too late. By then I'll have run out of air.*

Desperately I grasped the crowbar and pushed my feet against the door as I pried. It sprang open so suddenly that I was catapulted out into the open water on a cloud of silt, spinning out of control until I felt

102

hands hard on my arms, steadying me. I was staring wildly into another face mask. Bryan! He had come in time.

I was still staring, hardly believing my rescue, as he reached for my indicator, shook his head and, still grasping my arm, guided me away from the perilous slant of the deck and over the aft railing. I hung limply, allowing him to tow me to where the anchor rope rose, leading the way to safety.

The longing for fresh air and light, for freedom from the murky water, was almost unbearable. I wanted to fill my buoyancy vest and shoot up to the surface, gasp in real air; but Bryan's hand tight on my arm warned me. I nodded and began to rise slowly, no faster than the bubbles from my regulator. There wasn't a lot of time. My tank was almost empty and there was still the precautionary five-minutes wait at the fifteen-foot level.

I am going to run out of air, I thought in panic. But it was all right. Bryan rose level with me. He grasped the front of my vest and held out the extra regulator attached to his tank. Thankfully I removed my own mouthpiece and inserted the one he handed me. Sharing the air from his full tank, I hovered beside him. Face to face we waited in a strange forced intimacy. I could see his eyes, framed in his face mask. His jaw muscles tensed, clamping down on the mouthpiece of his regulator.

He must be furious. How am I going to explain?

Did he see what was in the cabin? No, there wasn't time.

How am I going to tell him?

I have to tell his father and Greg that I know. But Bryan?

And what about Amanda? How will she feel when she knows the truth?

Of course I must tell them. Didn't Dad and Mom and I plan all this to get at the truth? To find out exactly what happened to the little boy who vanished thirty years ago? My uncle. Mom's brother.

But. . .

I was jolted off the treadmill of my thoughts by Bryan's hand on my arm, his upraised thumb. Helplessly joined by the lifeline of air to this one special person whom I had conned and lied to, I rose to the surface.

Moonlight lay anchored on the sunny lake, the runabout tied astern. I had never seen anything so wonderful, except perhaps for the sun dancing on the water. Amanda grabbed my weight belt and then helped me aboard the launch.

"You're alive. You're okay." Her face was swollen with tears. "How *could* you? You said ten, fifteen minutes at the most."

I pulled off my mask and put my arms around her, holding her tight. "I know. I'm so sorry. Things went wrong."

I felt my buoyancy vest with its empty cylinder being unfastened and lifted off me. "Wrong?" Bryan said from behind me. His voice was choked with fury. "Do you realize that in another few minutes you'd have been dead?"

I was on the verge of tears, but I swallowed them down and managed a shaky laugh. "Oh, yes, I realize *that* all right. I'm sorry. I was stupid. I didn't think to fasten the door open. But I had to do it."

"Not good enough. If Amanda hadn't signalled me, you'd still be down there. Do you understand?" His hands were tight on my arms. Even through the thickness of neoprene I could feel the bite of his fingers. He shook me. "Do you?" he repeated.

"Of course I understand." I swallowed. "I'm sorry. And thank you for rescuing me."

"And that's it? Why on earth did you go back? We had the bell. We'd done what we set out to do."

I shrugged myself free of his hands. Anger was easier to deal with than guilt. "You mean *you* had the bell. *You'd* done what you had set out to do. Not me. The bell wasn't part of *my* agenda." I found I was trembling. *Just reaction. It's over now,* I told myself.

But was it? I still hadn't made up my mind how to use the evidence tucked in the pocket of my vest. My legs wobbled and I collapsed onto one of the benches. My small spurt of anger seemed to have drained from me the little energy I had left. Amanda helped Bryan out of his gear and hauled up the anchor. Bryan started the engine and we made our way back to the shore, the runabout bobbing on its towline behind us, Bryan grim and stony-faced at the tiller.

Amanda put her arms round me. "He doesn't mean it," she whispered. "It's just that he was so afraid that you . . . Well, you know."

"I know." I hugged Amanda back. "You're the one who should be mad at me. You're the one I really let down. I'm so sorry I scared you."

"I had to let Bryan know."

"Of course you did. You saved my life, truly. If there's ever anything I can do to repay that—"

"Yes, there sure is." Amanda's voice was urgent. "You can tell us what you're up to. What do you mean by your 'agenda'?"

chapter SIX

WHAT DO YOU mean by your 'agenda'?

I had managed to turn aside Amanda's question as we returned to the dock, but later, alone for a moment in the bedroom I shared with her, it came back to haunt me.

I was standing by the window, looking down over the trees to the sparkling lake, absently passing the medal and chain from hand to hand. The sun was low and the lake was tinged with crimson.

Blackened, almost unrecognizable as a piece of jewellery, the medal bore in low relief an image of Saint Christopher. Christopher: the name of Mom's younger brother. Also the patron saint of travellers and of safe journeys, I recalled with a grimace. Chris's last journey had happened a long time ago, and it had been a horrifying one.

I rubbed my thumb over the medal, feeling the engraving on the other side, the inscription I already knew by heart: CHRISTOPHER STEVEN HENDERSON. July 25, 1962. A baptismal gift from his godfather. And now proof, if I chose to use it, of the kidnapping, possibly the manslaughter, of an eight-year-old boy and of a conspiracy to conceal a body. Heavy charges, all of them. My hand closed around the chain, holding it tightly. What should I do?

The door burst open, and I jumped and turned away from the window. Amanda beamed in the doorway Obviously, as far as she was concerned, I was forgiven.

"*Here* you are! I've been helping Mom in the kitchen. We're going to have a totally splendid dinner, a real celebration, though she doesn't know what it's about yet. I just said we had a wonderful surprise in store for Dad. We're planning to keep everything a secret until it's time for dessert, and then—ta-dah!—the entrance of the bell on the cushion, like I said. What do you think? Bry's going to play a fanfare on the piano." She frowned. "It's too bad we don't have a trumpet. That'd be absolutely tops."

This was it, then. In a couple of hours I would be saying goodbye to Treetops, to Margaret's wonderful cooking, to the lake. To Amanda. To Bryan.

I slipped the chain into my pocket and forced a smile. "I hope the surprise goes well." I looked at my watch. "Six o'clock. I guess I'll also be celebrating my last night at Treetops. I must phone my parents—they'll be expecting a call—and arrange for them to pick me up tomorrow morning."

The glow left Amanda's face. "Do you have to go? You've hardly been here any time. Only eight days. Can't you stay a bit longer? *Please.*"

I shook my head. "Bryan's done what he set out to do. He no longer needs a diving buddy. And he certainly won't want to see me any more, that's obvious. I should be on my way. Places to go, things to do," I added lightly.

"Sandra, you're not leaving 'cause Bry was mad at you, are you? He didn't mean it, you know. He was just scared because of what might have happened. He likes you a whole bunch. Oh, please stay."

"I really want both of you to be my friends. But . . . well, I have a feeling you'll probably change your mind

107

about me before the evening's over. It'll all be different."
I clutched the medal in my pocket so hard that it bit
into my palm. "Now I *must* use the phone before Mom
and Dad go out for dinner."

I phoned the hotel on the list Mom had given me,
thankful that they weren't too far away. It was quite
possible, I realized ruefully, that the MacDonalds would
want me to leave immediately, once I'd told them what
I knew. *If* indeed I did tell them. I could still back away
from that final disclosure. We could say goodbye as
friends. But that would be the end. The terrible secret
would always lie between us, spoiling any contact in the
future. Oh, what should I do?

I could hear the hotel front desk ringing their room.
Then, thankfully, Mom's voice. "It's me," I managed to
say before tears sprang into my eyes and I choked up.

"Dearest girl, I'm so glad to hear from you. I can't
think why, but I've had an edgy feeling all day that
something was wrong. Are you all right?"

I swallowed and rubbed my hand impatiently over my
eyes. I managed to get out the necessary words. "It's all
right now, Mom. It's over." My voice shook only a little.

"Oh, my dear! Can you talk freely?"

"I'm not sure. Perhaps not." There were extensions
around the house, Greg might be listening and Amanda
was hovering excitedly outside the bedroom door. "But
I can tell you that I'm through here."

"Were you . . . successful?"

"Yes. Proof positive." There was silence at the other
end. "Mom?"

I heard Mom's uncertain laugh. "How odd that I
should want to mourn again after all these years. But
perhaps it's healthy. Closure."

"Is closure for *you* enough? Do you want me to—to go ahead here? Or should I keep quiet and leave it for you to follow up officially later—if you decide to?"

"Hold on." I could hear Mom and Dad talking in the distance. I clutched the phone hard. Then Mom's voice. "If it's safe for you . . . If you're not in any danger . . . ?" Her voice faded, and I remembered the very real danger I had been in, from which Bryan had rescued me. Then Mom spoke again. "Dad suggests you play it by ear—just see what happens."

I groaned inwardly. I'd hoped that Mom and Dad would make the decision for me. But here I was, stuck with it.

"We'll pick you up tomorrow morning. Around ten o'clock suit you? At the top of their driveway, if that's all right. I . . . I don't think I could bear to meet them."

"Okay, Mom. If they decide to kick me out tonight I'll call you back. Stay close."

"We will. And Sandra . . . thank you from the bottom of my heart."

I was just putting the phone down when Amanda bounced in. "Have you finished your call? You're really going? Oh, dear, I wish . . . Anyway, since we're celebrating tonight, we're going to dress up a bit. Come on. It's almost dinnertime."

She chatted merrily all the time we were changing, but afterwards I couldn't remember a word of what she'd said, or how I'd responded—and I suppose I must have spoken, since she didn't comment on my silence.

Margaret had done us proud. The table glistened with crystal and silver. Tantalizing smells wafted from the kitchen, but I realized with a twinge of nausea that I had absolutely no appetite. They had planned a celebration, but to me it seemed more like a funeral feast, or the last meal of a condemned prisoner. I would have given anything to be back with Mom and Dad in my ordinary, everyday world.

Maybe I'm wrong, I argued with myself. *Maybe they didn't know. Maybe Uncle Chris smuggled himself aboard and it was all a ghastly accident. But that doesn't account for Don's MacDonald's reaction to the tolling bell. Nor Greg's behaviour . . .* I felt in the pocket of my flowered dress for the silver medal and chain. *I guess I'll just have to see it through—and watch for their reactions.*

At the sound of the dinner bell everyone gathered in the dining room: the senior Mrs. MacDonald, her sons and Bryan. Amanda and Margaret passed out bowls of soup, which were followed by a salad and then by an exotic chicken dish. Among the adults the conversation moved smoothly. Bryan, when asked, talked about the dives without saying anything important. Amanda was unusually quiet, though bursting with ill-concealed excitement. She jumped up to fetch extra butter, again to refill the water glasses.

"You're like a grasshopper on a hot plate," her grand-mother exclaimed. "What's got into you, child?"

"Nothing, Gran. Sorry." But though she sat quietly afterwards, she still looked incandescent.

I don't want to put out that light, I thought as I forced myself to eat, crumbling my roll, pushing my food around the plate, answering automatically when spoken to.

The only exchange I remembered afterwards took place when Amanda brought in dessert plates and a wonderfully elaborate English trifle in a cut-glass bowl.

"So, Cassandra," Greg suddenly addressed me. "You've been very silent all evening. Any dire prophecies to share with us?"

I felt a cold shiver run down my back. I managed a smile. "Not at the moment. But remember, Greg, my namesake's tragedy was that nobody believed her—not until it was too late."

Greg laughed and Amanda looked puzzled. The trifle was spooned out and the plates handed round.

"Delicious, my dear Margaret," remarked the senior Mrs. MacDonald. "What an excellent cook you are. Is this magnificence celebrating some special event? I'm puzzled. Have I forgotten someone's birthday? Or an anniversary? I *do* hope not."

"It's a surprise of the children's, Mother," Margaret replied, and as if on cue, Amanda jumped up.

"Ready, Bry?"

"Let me know when to start." Bryan went to the piano, saying over his shoulder, "You have to pretend this is a trumpet, folks. As in a fanfare."

Amanda's feet thudded down the stairs. I looked around at the tolerant smiles on the faces of the adults. An amusement of the children's, nothing more, they clearly thought. I watched, waiting tensely to see whose face would change. I could hear Amanda coming upstairs now, walking more slowly. "Now, Bry!" she called.

Bryan played a noisy and triumphant set of chords on the piano and then came back to stand beside his father as Amanda entered the room, carrying the bell on its red cushion. Carefully she placed it in front of her father. "Ta-dah!" She stood back, watching him eagerly.

There was a frozen moment, like a bizarre family

photograph, that I knew would remain in my memory forever. Amanda standing to the right of her father, Bryan to his left. Don staring at the bell, his linen table napkin clutched in his left hand, the colour draining slowly from his face till it was almost as white as the cloth. Greg's face blank, all emotion wiped off it. Margaret and her mother-in-law looking mildly interested.

For a long, agonizing moment no one spoke. Then Don croaked, "What . . . ?" He licked his pale lips and took a gulp of water. "What?" he repeated.

"Don't you see, Daddy? The name's still on the side, almost as clear as ever. *Far Skimmer*. Isn't it amazing? We found the sloop, and Bry and Sandra brought the bell up this morning."

"So now you won't have to listen to it ringing every time there's a storm, Dad," Bryan explained.

"'Tolling' is the word you want, Bry," Greg said. "As in 'tolling for the dead.'"

"Damn you, Greg! Shut up!" Don's face turned from white to red.

Mrs. MacDonald frowned. "I won't have you using such language, if you please, Don, especially in front of the children. I'm surprised at you. But I don't under-stand. Have the children actually found the wreck of *Far Skimmer*? Dear me, it must have been down there for thirty years. Why are you so upset, Don? You should be grateful. You won't be reminded of that terrible wreck every time there's a storm. You should thank Bryan for going to all this trouble. And it's a very *hand-some* bell."

Greg began to laugh hysterically. "A handsome bell! Oh, Mother, how priceless! If you only knew!"

"Stop it, Greg!" Don slammed his fist on the table,

spilling his wine in a pool of red across the white cloth.

Margaret stared in bewilderment at her husband. "Don? What is it? What's wrong?"

Bryan's expression mirrored his mother's. "*Dad?* I thought you'd be so pleased. It's like . . . exorcising a ghost, isn't it?"

I felt a mixture of pity and guilt as I looked at Bryan's puzzled face. *Maybe I should have told him my suspicions earlier—but how could I? Would he even have believed me? Either way, our friendship's at an end*, I thought sadly. *As dead as the child in the saloon of* Far Skimmer.

Don stood up so abruptly that his chair caught in the rug and fell on its side. His mother looked over her glasses at him. "Sit down at once, Donald, and control yourself. Bryan and Amanda, you will also please be seated. Now"—she looked around the table—"Donald, will you kindly explain what this uncalled-for emotional display is all about?"

"Mother, I can't . . . not here, not now."

"Greg?" She turned to her second son. He shook his head, his face still blank.

"You have nothing to say, either of you?" Mrs. MacDonald sighed and lightly beat the table with her fist. "Nothing has been the same between you two boys since the day *Far Skimmer* went down. It's as if you've been haunted by it. But why? All three of you were saved. No harm was done, except for the loss of your father's yacht. So what *is* this all about? Whatever the mystery is, it has gone on quite long enough—too long, in fact. I demand an explanation."

"For God's sake, Mother, no!"

"There you go again, all fired up over a simple question.

And I've already asked you to curb your language, Donald. I would like a straightforward answer, with no prevarication, please."

Margaret broke the silence that followed. "Answer her, Don, please. For my sake, answer *me*. Mother used the word *haunted*, and it's so true. I *love* Treetops. In spite of its inconvenience and its size and its distance from any decent stores, I wouldn't want to live anywhere else. But ever since your father died and left you the house, it's as if you've been split in two. Half of you would like to leave tomorrow and never come back. The other half seems to be tied here. Isn't that so, Don?"

Her husband didn't answer but stared grimly in front of him, his hands gripping the table.

"Tied to the house? Or to *Far Skimmer*? Is that what you mean, Margaret? It all sounds very far-fetched." Mrs. MacDonald's voice was crisp.

Margaret flushed. "It's the truth, Mother. I know how much Don has changed—more than you would know, I suppose. Nothing's been the same since we came back to live at Treetops. But he won't talk about it. He just retreats into his shell and plays his everlasting Wagner every time there's a storm. It's as if—"

"But don't you see, Mom?" Amanda interrupted. "He won't have to do that any more. That's what Bry planned. That's why he spent the summer at the dive sites looking for a diving buddy, so he could find *Far Skimmer* and get the bell. And now he's done it and Dad's free. Don't you see?"

"*I* see, my dear. But does your father?"

As I watched the drama from my end of the table, I saw Bryan and Amanda stare at their father and then look at each other, the disappointment and bewilder-

114

ment written clearly on their faces. Again I felt a twinge of guilt at having helped to bring about this terrible scene. I swallowed, steeling myself against the knowledge that the worst was still to come.

Don sat silently, his face drawn, unconsciously twisting his napkin in his hands. Greg's face was as impenetrable as a stone statue's, his eyes two grey pebbles. With his right hand he played idly with his wineglass, slowly twirling the fluted stem between his fingers. He was the key to the whole mystery, I was sure.

"Greg." I spoke abruptly, my own voice startling me. I hadn't intended to say my thought out loud. Everyone—except Greg—turned to stare at me. I swallowed and went on. "Everyone asks Don about *Far Skimmer*. But you were aboard the day of the accident too, weren't you, Greg? Perhaps we should ask you for *your* memories of that day. Maybe you could tell us what actually happened, and why it has upset your brother so much more than you."

Greg's hand was still. He didn't look at me, nor at anyone else, though everyone's eyes were on him. He gave a forced laugh. "I have no idea what you're driving at. *Far Skimmer* and that wretched bell mean nothing to me. It's all in the past."

"Oh, Uncle Greg, what a whopper!"

"Amanda, that's not nice. Apologize to your uncle," Margaret exclaimed.

"But it *is* a lie, Mom. Look." She marked off her points on her fingers. "He invited himself here as soon as he knew Bry had found a diving partner, even though he hadn't been down here in *months and months*. He spied on us when we were out in *Moonlight*. We saw the place on the headland where he'd been watching us.

115

Then he took off in *Moonlight,* with all our diving gear aboard, so we couldn't go out. After the storm, when Bry and Sandra were diving, he came buzzing around in the runabout, totally ignoring our diving flag, and he wouldn't quit till I threatened to call the police on the radio."

"He also made up a story about my parents phoning, to try to delay us till he could come aboard and see what we were up to," I added.

"Cassandra, Cassandra, you told me that your name-sake's warnings were never believed. These stories won't be believed either. They're just not credible. The children have been playing imaginative games, Mother, and have gotten carried away. I repeat, *Far Skimmer* means nothing to me."

"Now you've gone too far, little brother." Don's voice, after his long silence, startled us all. He rubbed his hands over his face as if his skin were frozen, and looked around at us. "The truth is that Greg's been blackmailing me for years. Ever since Dad died and left me Treetops and the money." His voice was grim.

The two brothers glared at each other. Physically they were alike in bone structure and colouring, but now their faces were like two contrary masks. Don's was pale and drawn, Greg's was flushed, his features suddenly coarse.

I didn't allow myself to look away from the two men for an instant. I heard their mother's disbelieving cry of "Greg?" and Margaret's "Oh, Don, no!" and I knew I could not conceal the evidence I had taken from the cabin. Nothing but the truth would serve now. *And the truth shall make you free.*

I put my right hand into the pocket of my cotton dress

and drew out the medal and chain. I hadn't tried to clean them. I dropped them to the table in front of me, a small blackened heap.

"What's that?" Amanda asked.

"It's a Saint Christopher medal on a silver chain. I found it on the floor of the cabin on *Far Skimmer*."

"That's why you went back," Bryan exclaimed. "That's why you risked diving alone. For a *medal*. But—"

"How did you know it would be there?" Amanda asked suddenly. "And whose is it?"

"Whose *was* it. It belonged to my uncle Chris. My mother's younger brother. He disappeared thirty years ago. The family was on holiday on the other side of the lake. He'd had a fight with his dad and gone down to the marina on his own. He was never seen again. At first they thought he must have fallen off the dock and drowned. But nobody saw it happen, and though that part of the lake was dragged, his body was never found."

I paused and looked around. The senior Mrs. MacDonald was staring at me with eyes that were wide and dark with horror, as if she already knew how the story must end. Neither Don nor Greg looked at me or at each other. I went on reluctantly, forcing out each word.

"There was a rumour, never substantiated, that he'd been playing with two boys a few years older than he was—he had just had his eighth birthday. But the story came to nothing. The only boys anyone could identify as being around that day were the sons of Michael MacDonald, a highly respected citizen, a man above reproach. He swore he knew nothing about the lost boy, and when the two children were tracked down and interviewed at their Toronto school, they also denied any knowledge of him. It was a dead end. There was no real evidence, only rumour. Even the family yacht, *Far Skimmer*, was no more. For that was the day of the storm, the day she foundered on a shoal."

Greg shook his head. "Oh, Cassandra, what a story. To my knowledge I never met any boy around that time called Christopher."

Don looked up. For an instant a wild hope flashed across his face. "That's true."

I shook my head. "The name engraved on the medal is Christopher *Steven* Henderson. And the birth date is correct: July 25, 1962. He never liked being called Christopher, my mother told me. He thought it was too sissy. He used to call himself Steve, even though the family insisted on Christopher."

"*Steve!*" The word was wrung out of Don like a cry for help.

"Shut up, you fool," snarled Greg.

"No, brother. It's too late for silence now. It's time for the truth. At last. Thirty years too late. But at last—the truth."

chapter SEVEN

"HE TOLD US his name was Steve," Don explained. "Later, when it was announced over the radio that a boy called Christopher was missing, we thought—that is, we tried to fool ourselves into believing—that it had never happened." He ran his hands through his hair. "It's impossible to explain how we could do something like that. When something in your life is so bad that you can't bear to look at it, to think about it, then you grasp at straws."

"But when you saw his photograph in the papers, on TV," Bryan accused his father, "you must have known then it was the same boy."

"We didn't have the newspaper delivered back then. And no TV. There was just the radio and the story of a kid called Christopher. So we said nothing. We did nothing."

"But he was aboard *Far Skimmer*," Bryan persisted. "Sandra has the proof. You must have known—"

"She has a medal and chain she *says* she found aboard the yacht. And we've only got her word for that. So keep your mouth shut, Don," Greg interrupted.

"Thank you for your advice, Greg. But I've gone along with suppressing the truth for far too many years. And the cost has been too high, both in guilt and in the amount you've bled from me as the price of my silence."

"Uncle Greg, is it true what Dad said? Have you been blackmailing him?" Bryan looked stricken.

"Nonsense, Bryan. He's helped me out of trouble in

one or two failed ventures. Nothing to do with *Far Skimmer*, or with a missing boy. Your father's exaggerating as usual." He turned to his brother, his voice suddenly hard. "Be quiet, Don. A medal proves nothing. Nothing at all."

"How about it, Sandra?" Bryan's voice was accusing, and I couldn't help flinching. *I've found the truth I hunted for. But in exchange I've lost a good friend. Someone special.* Yet my loss was nothing compared with Bryan's and Amanda's, I told myself. They'd lost respect for their father.

"You came here as a spy, didn't you?" he insisted. "Just to worm out our family secrets. When I invited you to be my diving partner, you never told me you already knew about us. When I told you my plan to bring up the bell, you never said that you suspected Dad. You went along with the exploration, like a friend, until I found *Far Skimmer*. Then you stole off on your own, without a word to me. You've no witness to your dive. Amanda couldn't see what you were up to. How do I know if you really found anything? Maybe Uncle Greg's right. Maybe you brought that medal with you. Maybe you never found it on the yacht at all. Maybe this is just a plot to make trouble for our family. Publicity, is that it? Or money to buy our silence?"

This was worse than I had expected. I looked at him dumbly, my one-time friend. How could he believe for one instant that my motives were so sleazy?

"That's not true, Bry!" Amanda burst out. "Sandra wouldn't lie to us, would you, Sandra?"

I shook my head. "I didn't lie. Not exactly . . ."

"Maybe not in *words*," Bry put in, "but in intention. In

not telling us who you were. You deceived us then, so why should I believe anything you say now?"

"I'm sorry I deceived you, Bryan. I didn't want to, only I didn't think you'd believe me, not without proof. But what I have said is the truth. I *did* find the medal in the cabin. And that wasn't all. The rest'll be easy enough to prove, I'm afraid. I found—"

I stopped and took a sip of water, my mouth suddenly dry. My hand shook, spilling water on the tablecloth. "I found the bones of a young boy. As far as I could tell the skull is intact. Dental records will prove definitely whether the body is that of my uncle or not."

I looked up to see horrified eyes staring at me. Margaret moaned, "Don! This can't be true, can it?" Her clasped hands went to her mouth.

Mrs. MacDonald frowned at her daughter-in-law. "Hush, Margaret. No hysteria, please. Let me get this quite clear, Sandra. You're saying there is a dead body aboard the old yacht?"

"Yes, Mrs. MacDonald. I'm sorry, but that's the truth."

"And you believe it to be the body of your uncle, the child who went missing thirty years ago?"

I nodded.

"And my boys . . ." Mrs. MacDonald stumbled over the words and then continued, her voice steady. "Don and Greg were responsible for what happened? Only them? Don't tell me their father knew!"

I looked at her frankly. "I don't know. It seems likely that Don and Greg alone were responsible. But only they can tell you."

"And so they shall." Mrs. MacDonald tightened her lips. "I want to hear the whole story—the true story, please. From you first, Don. Then from Greg."

"There's nothing to tell, Mother," Greg insisted.

"Oh, Greg, it's too late to go on lying." Don turned almost eagerly to his mother, as if he were at last ridding himself of an intolerable burden. "This is what happened, Mother. It was a fine morning, near the end of the holidays. Father had a business meeting with someone, and he took Greg and me across the lake for the ride. We had lunch at the marina, and then Father went off to his appointment, leaving us on board. I remember we'd bought some comics and snacks and we were down in the saloon. After a time, I don't remember how long, the wind got up and *Far Skimmer* began to lurch at her moorings. It got kind of uncomfortable below, so we went up on deck. That's when we saw the kid. He was just hanging around, looking up at *Far Skimmer*. You could tell he was wishing it was his. So Greg invited him on board—"

"I did not, Mother. It was Don."

"I will listen to your story later, Greg. Go on, Donald."

"As I was saying, Greg asked him on board. He was showing off a bit, as if it was *our* yacht, not Father's. He showed the kid all over, boasting about the places *Far Skimmer* had been, as if we'd been along on those trips too, instead of only sailing her on the lakes."

"Not so! It was you—"

"The kid was wild to go for a spin. I remember asking him, 'Where are your mom and dad?' and he said that he was fed up with them and was running away. 'It's no fun being the second kid,' he said. 'They let her do all sorts of stuff and say I'm too young. If I could sail on a boat like this, I'd really show them.' Something like that."

Is that where the tragedy began? I wondered. *With*

something as small as jealousy between brother and sister over nothing important at all?

"That's when the idea of letting the kid stow away came up."

"You didn't kidnap him?"

"Of course not, Mother. We weren't criminals," Don snapped. Then his face crumpled and he put his hands up to cover it. "What am I saying? We *are* criminals. Not *then*. But ever since."

"Who had the idea of helping the child to stow away, Don?" his mother prompted.

"I don't remember. It was one of those things that kind of escalated. A joke, that's all. We worked out that we'd hide him aboard until we were more than halfway home, and then it would be too late to turn back. Surprise Father, you know?"

"So that's what the two of you did?"

"Yes. We planned to hide Steve—Christopher—in the saloon until we were well out on the lake. But the weather was getting pretty rough by the time Father got down to the marina from his business appointment, and when we saw him running towards the dock, we could see he was wet through. It was raining steadily by then, and we knew he'd want to change before heading home. So . . ." He faltered.

"Go on, Donald."

"So we hid the kid in one of the lockers under the couch. Some blankets were stored in it, but we pushed them into one of the other lockers to make room for him. He thought it was a great joke. Then we got into our rain gear and life jackets and went up on deck just as Father came aboard. He was in a devil of a hurry. Started the engine right away and cast off. It wasn't until we were clear of the marina that he told us the weather office had issued a storm warning, that a big blow was coming behind the rain. He had me take the helm and sent Greg up into the bow to keep an eye out for other vessels while he went below to get changed. The visibility was already pretty bad."

"Why in the world didn't you tell your father right then that you'd taken on a passenger?"

"It all happened so fast, I guess we just didn't think. You have no idea what it was like, Mother. The wind and waves. Father barking out orders. 'Don't chatter. Just do what I tell you.' *You* know. He had us jumping. Then he came up in his rain gear and a life jacket. He looked over to the southwest, where the weather was coming from, and said he'd put up a bit of sail, not too much, just enough to get us quickly across the lake before the worst of the storm hit. He had me continue steering while he hoisted the sail and trimmed it. Then he called Greg to come back from the bow and he made us both sit in the lee of the cabin while he took over the steering. The wind was pretty well behind us by now and we made good time sailing across the lake. Father was a great sailor—well, you know that, Mother—and I never for a moment thought we wouldn't make it, but it was still a frightening experience. We sat tight and said nothing—just watched Father handling the steering and the sail."

"You must have thought about the boy then? Didn't you worry that he might be scared below on his own? And I suppose he didn't even have a life jacket on."

"We weren't thinking about *anything*, Mother. It was like a roller coaster, both exciting and terrifying. Greg and I were just hanging on while *Far Skimmer* leapt through the waves and the wind screamed in our ears. I never once thought about the kid. Not till later. The storm got worse and worse. I remember once I yelled to Father, 'Shouldn't we turn back?' and he shook his head, saying something about the wind behind us being the only thing in our favour."

"I know just what you mean, Dad," Amanda said comfortingly. "I remember once losing my bus pass and not even having money for a phone call, and I was so scared I couldn't think of a thing. I just went blank."

"Thanks, Amanda. But what we did—or rather didn't do—was a lot more serious." Her father gave a tired smile. "Your grandfather was amazing. It was as if he and *Far Skimmer* were one. He yelled at us to look out for buoys, so I knew we had to be getting close to the north shore, though I had no idea of the time. But we couldn't see a thing, what with the sudden darkness of the storm and the spray blowing off the tops of the waves. Father ran down the sail, but we were still going at a fair clip when we hit the shoal. We didn't stop dead—I suppose if we had, we'd have been tossed into the water and that would have been the end of us. The end of the MacDonald dynasty." He stopped and looked at Bryan and Amanda before going on.

"There was a terrible grinding noise and *Far Skimmer* shuddered and slowed down. Almost at once she began to list to port, and we knew we'd never make it to dry land in her. Father cut the engine and got the dinghy over the side with two lines holding it. I remember it slapping up and down, tossing around. He picked us up, one by one, and dropped us in. Then he scrambled in after us, started the engine and cast off the lines. That was honestly the first moment I remembered the kid."

I could see that his face was shiny with sweat. He wiped it with his napkin and went on.

"I wondered afterwards, why didn't he come up from the cabin when it got really rough? Or when we started shipping water? Water must have been pouring into the cabin. He had been in one of the lockers, as I said. They had spring fittings so they wouldn't swing open during a blow, and for a horrible moment I thought, *Maybe he's trapped in there.* But you can easily push them open from inside. I remember Greg and I playing hide-and-seek in there when we were little and it was never a problem."

He stopped talking and gulped water. He wiped his face again.

"Why didn't you tell your father *then* that Chris was still aboard?" I burst out.

He shook his head. "I don't know, Sandra. We were wallowing through the waves, making almost no headway, taking in water. Father yelled at us to use the bailer, so I unfastened it and began scooping the water over the side almost as fast as it was coming in. When I was tired Greg took over and I tried bailing with my hands. I didn't think . . . but I don't believe there was any way we could have turned back anyway. *I'll tell him when we get ashore,* I thought. *If we get ashore.* I remember the enormous feeling of relief when I felt the gravel grate under the keel and knew we'd made it. We scrambled up through the woods to the highway and after a while a passing driver gave us a lift home."

"You were like drowned rats," Mrs. MacDonald said. "I remember the water pouring off you as if you'd had to swim ashore. And as cold as ice cubes." She turned to me. "I could tell they'd only just made it. They were dazed and shivering. I got the three of them out of their clothes and under hot showers. I heated up some soup and got the boys into bed, bundled together for warmth. Meanwhile their father phoned the police to report the sinking of *Far Skimmer*, with no loss of life."

"And you still said nothing?" I asked Don.

He shook his head. "Not to the grown-ups, Sandra. We were in bed, shivering, clutching each other. And I said, 'What about the kid? What about Steve?' And Greg said, 'What kid?' I remember staring at him, and he looked back at me with his eyes kind of blank. For a minute I thought he *really* had forgotten. Then he said, 'You mean the kid on the dock? You think maybe he snuck aboard when we weren't looking? Too bad for him if he did.' Then he turned on his side and went to sleep. Or maybe he just pretended to. I lay awake for the longest time, imagining the kid getting out of the locker and finding the cabin knee-deep in water, the yacht heeling over, the water pouring in. Thinking of him trapped down there, not able to get out. And then I thought, *Maybe he came up on deck earlier and we never saw him. That way he'd have been swept off by a wave. A quick death rather than a slow one.* And I prayed that that was what had happened."

"*Oh, Dad.*" Amanda pushed her chair back and ran around the table to hug her father.

He pushed her gently away. "Don't, Amanda. I don't deserve your pity."

"But . . ."

"Sit down, dear," Mrs. MacDonald said quietly but firmly. I looked at the older woman. Her face was stern, and she seemed to show no emotion. But then I saw her jaw stiffen and her throat muscles move as she swallowed. Her hands were on the table, lightly clenched. She turned to her younger son. "Well, Greg, does your account of what happened agree with Don's?"

Greg hesitated, and it seemed to me that he was considering denying the whole affair. I wondered if he was going to suggest that Christopher had snuck aboard and stowed away without their knowledge. But if he were to deny *that* knowledge, then his blackmail of Don made no sense.

He must have come to the same conclusion. He shrugged. "It was his responsibility to look after the kid. Don was the one who asked him aboard."

"That's a black lie, Greg!"

"Be quiet, Donald. You've had your turn. It's Greg's now. Did *you* remember the boy after *Far Skimmer* foundered?"

He shook his head. "Don's telling the truth there. It all happened so fast. You've got to remember that I was just a little kid, two years younger than Don. Makes a big difference at that age. I looked up to him, you know. Went along with his schemes."

I saw Greg's face change subtly as he spoke. His eyes widened and took on a innocent look.

I heard Amanda whisper, "Slime!" under her breath.

Don slammed his hand down on the table. "Mother, are you going to listen to him? You can't trust a word he says."

Mrs. MacDonald sighed. "I certainly can't recall any occasion on which you hero-worshipped Don or went along with any of his schemes, Greg. Is that all you have to say?"

I broke in. "What happened afterwards? There was an inquiry, of course."

"Not into the loss of *Far Skimmer*, because there were no other craft involved," Mrs. MacDonald said. "She foundered fairly close to shore, out of the regular shipping lanes. As I said, my husband reported it to the police and that was the end of it. A few days later the boys went back to school and their father to the office, while I closed up the house for the winter."

"But the police *did* investigate Christopher's disappearance. I know they talked to the boys as well as your husband," I protested.

"If you know that, you know they were not able to help . . ." She faltered. "That is to say, the boys were interviewed at school and told the police that they hadn't seen the missing child. That was the end of it."

I couldn't contain my frustration. "It's unbelievable. People saw him near *Far Skimmer*, but the police never pursued it further!" *Money, power, influence*, I thought bitterly. Right at that moment I despised the whole family, Bryan included.

"I know my husband never saw the child. The boys said they hadn't either—and no one had any reason to believe they were lying." She looked at me bleakly. "What can I say? It seems we were wrong. I'm so sorry."

"And the boys never gave anything away? They never seemed to you to be—well—*burdened* by some kind of secret?"

She shook her head. "Not then."

There was silence for a minute. Don tried to explain. "It's not so hard to forget something horrible when you're young. To push it out of your head. It was only later, as an adult, that it all came back to haunt me."

"Dad, what I want to know is why you decided to live at Treetops all year round. I suppose it wouldn't have been too difficult to forget what happened when you were in Toronto. But back here, with the lake outside, and the bell tolling in storms, reminding you . . . How *could* you?" Amanda's voice was shrill.

"I didn't have any choice, kitten. When your grandfather died, he left this house to me and a generous bequest for its upkeep. He'd always loved Treetops and was very proud of it, even though he'd only used it as a summer home. Then Greg. . ." He hesitated and I saw his face harden. "Then Greg began to blackmail me about the boy."

"You don't mean that literally, do you, Don?" I saw Mrs. MacDonald suddenly lose her composure. Don didn't answer, but his grim expression told the truth. She pressed her hands against her trembling lips. "Oh, it's too much. Did your father and I not raise you to be *honourable* men?"

"*One* mistake, Mother. One lie that led to other lies. I was a kid and I was scared. I thought they might send us to prison. So I pushed it out of my mind. And I was fairly successful. For some twenty years I managed to forget it."

"If only you and your brother had trusted your father and me with the truth."

Don gave a humourless laugh. "If only. Oh, Mother, life is full of 'if onlys,' isn't it? Some more tragic and ghastly than others."

"You haven't really answered Amanda's question, Dad." Bryan's face was pale, and I saw that he didn't look at his father when he spoke to him. "Why did you go on staying here when the lake, the storms, especially the bell, reminded you of what had happened?"

"As I said, Greg began asking me for money. Oh, he

didn't call it blackmail— did you, dear brother? I was just helping him bail out his foundering business deals, one after another. But he got greedier, to the point where I couldn't keep both the Toronto house *and* Treetops. With the Rosedale house sold I could afford to support Greg without hurting Margaret and the children."

"Uncle Greg, how could you do that to Dad?" Amanda cried.

"Indeed. How could you? A son of mine?"

Greg pouted. *Like a child*, I thought, *not grown-up at all*. "Father always favoured Don, you know that, Mother. Leaving him Treetops and the major part of his estate was the last straw. I'd been counting on some of that money. I'd borrowed on that expectation—so when Father died, I was in trouble. I only asked Don for a fair share of what was rightfully mine."

"Asked? If you'd come to me as brother to brother, instead of threatening me . . ." Don frowned.

"I don't see why you gave in to his threats, Dad. He would have implicated himself just as much as you if he'd told the police what happened that day."

Don shook his head. "It's not that simple, Bryan. A scandal of any kind, with the appalling publicity and people's loss of confidence would have ruined me—I'm a stockbroker after all. I handle a great deal of money for important clients. Greg, on the other hand—" He broke off and shrugged his shoulders.

"What your father means is that your Uncle Greg is just a failed salesman, kiddies. A scandal wouldn't have hurt me in the same way."

"Enough." Mrs. MacDonald clapped her hands together. "Don, what do you intend to do about this now?"

"Inform the police. Accept whatever comes." He sighed. "What else *can* I do? Except for the most difficult thing of all," he said, looking at me. "Apologize to the family of . . . of Christopher. What they choose to do is up to them."

"Your mother is Christopher's sister, Sandra? Are there other relatives?"

I nodded. "My grandparents are still alive. They don't know that Dad and Mom and I have been trying to find the truth. It'll be up to Mom to tell them. The loss of their only son was a terrible blow. I don't think my grandmother ever quite got over it. And it affected Mom too. Not knowing was a nightmare for them. At first they thought he must have been kidnapped, and for days they waited for a ransom note. When that never came, they knew he had to be dead. Mom told me what that was like. Every time a body was found, they'd wait to find out the age, the sex, how long ago . . . On two occasions my grandfather had to go and see the remains himself. But of course it was never Christopher. Because Christopher was still aboard *Far Skimmer*."

"So that's why you tricked Bry into inviting you here. Well, I don't blame you, Sandra. Not a bit!"

"Thank you, Amanda." The tears were suddenly very close to the surface again. I pushed my chair back abruptly. "Please excuse me. I know it seems kind of shameful to have come here under false pretences, especially when you have all been so hospitable and welcoming. I'm sorry, but it's something I had to do. I had to lay Christopher to rest and give my mother a new life."

I didn't wait for a response but ran downstairs,

rubbing my hand across my eyes. I heard footsteps, and at the foot of the flight I turned. Bryan was just behind me with Amanda at his heels.

"Wait, Bry, don't!" Amanda called to him. He ignored her and grabbed me by the arm.

"Just how long were you spying on us before you trapped me into inviting you here?"

"Spying?" I twisted out of his grip and faced him. "I was only interested in finding the truth. Mother always suspected that *Far Skimmer* was the key to Uncle Chris's disappearance. Sure, I deliberately hung around and went on dives, hoping to meet you, angling for an invitation to Treetops."

Bryan glared at me and I looked steadily back, refusing to turn my eyes away. His face was white, and I could see a muscle in the corner of his jaw pulse.

"So you've been planning this the whole summer?"

I smiled wryly. "You have no idea, Bryan. It's been two years since Mom told me the whole story. Before that I only knew that Uncle Chris had died as a boy, and that Mom didn't like to talk about it. But when we moved house I found the newspaper accounts of the missing boy, and I got Mom to tell me the whole story. It obsessed her. She had a whole file full of clippings. She had found out everything she could about the MacDonald family, about the owner of *Far Skimmer* and about the famous house, Treetops. You were featured in so many magazines—it was hardly spying! One article spoke of the two sons, the ones who had told the police that they'd never seen Uncle Chris. And it mentioned the son and daughter of the present owner of Treetops. Even your names, Bryan and Amanda. It wasn't difficult. So Dad and Mom and I visited the area last summer. Asked around. Found out that you were a scuba diver. Found out you'd been looking for a diving buddy."

"You don't call that spying?"

"If it makes you happier, you can call it that. I don't really care," I snapped.

"Bry, stop it. Let Sandra explain."

I shrugged. "Anyway, that's when the plan developed. Last winter I learned how to scuba dive and decided to come up this summer and try to meet you."

"So devious. That's what I can't stomach. Why didn't your mother take her suspicions to the police?"

I gave a humourless laugh. "You still don't get it, do you? The police weren't interested in *Far Skimmer* or her wealthy owner thirty years ago. Why would they be interested now, after all this time? No, we had to get proof first. So I hung around the dock and asked the man taking the boat out if he knew you. I . . . ." I felt myself blushing and turned away. "I let the man think I was interested in you, and he was only too happy to play Cupid. I guess that *was* sneaky. But I was determined to help Mom find the truth, and that was the only way I could think of doing it."

"And I fell for it. What a dope!"

"You're being so unfair, Bry," Amanda argued. "If Sandra hadn't come, you'd never have found the bell, and you know you'd been planning that for ages."

"I wish I'd never had the stupid idea. What a can of worms I opened."

"I think finding out the truth is more important. And I think Dad'll be better off now the secret's out in the open. I just can't imagine how he must have felt all those years, with guilt just *eating* at him."

134

"That's a dopey movie kind of idea, Amanda. Use your head. Can you imagine what sort of meal the newspapers'll make of the story? 'Influential Bay Street broker a murderer.'"

"Now you're being ridiculous," I said. "He was never a murderer. It was a horrible accident, and the only things he and Greg did wrong were not telling your grandfather and then lying to the police. I think that if they make a clean breast of it now, there'll be very little fuss."

"You made a fool of me," Bryan muttered.

"Too bad. I'm sorry, but that's not important," I snapped, though I knew that it wasn't true. What Bryan thought of me would always be important. And I knew I would never forget him. The blond hair that tightened into curls when it was wet. The clear blue eyes that wrinkled at the corners when he smiled. The golden tan on his arms, the two small moles, like a colon, on the back of his right wrist.

Amanda shook Bryan's arm. "Bry, listen. You're making a fool of yourself. You know you were determined to get the bell. If it hadn't been Sandra, it would have been someone else. Or maybe you would have had to wait till I was old enough to dive with you."

"So?"

"So I don't believe you'd have let *Far Skimmer* just lie there once you'd found the bell. You'd have gone back. Your very own wreck to explore! Sure you would have. Sooner or later you'd have gone into the saloon. And then *you'd* have found Christopher." Amanda took a deep breath. "Think about *that*."

I saw Bryan open his mouth to argue and then shut it again. He shrugged. "Maybe you're right, Amanda. But

135

it doesn't change the fact that you cheated me, Sandra. You made me think . . ." He stopped, his cheeks red.

My hand closed over the medal in my pocket. *At least I've done what I came to do,* I told myself. *Why should I have expected to find a special friend as well? I'm no worse off than I was before.* But I knew that I was only fooling myself.

Aloud I said, "I'll phone my parents. They're expecting me. I'll have them come and pick me up tonight."

"Oh, Sandra, please stay."

I shook my head. "Thanks, Amanda. But I think it would be better for everyone if I left now. I'll call them and get packed up."

"I'll help you. As for you, Bry—you're horrid! Just see what you've done."

Bryan turned away.

"So where are you going now, Bry? To sulk some more?"

"No, Amanda. I'm going to tell Dad I'm sorry. To tell him this mess is my fault. I should have let *Far Skimmer* lie."

So Amanda helped me pack and then take my bag and diving gear up the driveway to wait for Mom and Dad. She tried so hard to be friendly, but there was no way she could understand the pain in my heart. I couldn't really understand it myself.

chapter EIGHT

. . . BUT WHEN Bry said that, about not looking for Far
Skimmer, *Dad told him not to blame himself. Letting* Far
Skimmer *stay wrecked with your poor uncle in it was a
far greater lie, he said. And you know what, Sandra, now
that the truth's come out, he's a different person. Well,
you saw him at the inquest, so I bet you noticed.*

I put down the letter from Amanda and looked out of
my bedroom window. In the park opposite the school
the leaves were beginning to turn. I did indeed remember the inquest, reliving the awful moment of telling the
coroner of my discovery of Christopher's bones and the
identifying medal. The press had been there, and once
the verdict of death by misadventure had been brought
in, Mom and I had been surrounded by questioning
reporters.

"I'm not seeking revenge," Mom had protested. "Only
closure. And we have that now. It is finished." And to
further questions then and later she would only shake
her head and say nothing.

Don and Greg MacDonald had been rebuked for not
telling the police that Christopher had been aboard *Far
Skimmer*, but since the accident had happened almost
thirty years before, when they were children, the case
had been closed. As Mom had said, it was finished. We
held a simple private ceremony, and buried
Christopher's remains in the family plot. The wreck of
Far Skimmer lay on the shoal where the yacht had

foundered. Out of shipping lanes and far beneath the lake, it was no hazard. Life went on . . .

We don't see Uncle Greg nowadays, which is just fine by me. Dad is so much happier, and of course he doesn't play Wagner during storms any more. Mom is happier too, not because of the Wagner, but because Dad is so different. They are actually planning a trip to Asia this winter—just the two of them—so I know things are better. And it's all thanks to you, Sandra. Do you remember saying that the truth makes you free? Something like that. Is that a quote from somewhere or did you make it up? It sure is true anyway. So thanks.

Lots of love from your friend Amanda.

P.S. I don't often see Bry now, since our schools are in different parts of Toronto, and he isn't much of a letter-writer—to his kid sister anyway. But Mom tells me that he's doing okay. I just wish he were still friends with you—that would be perfect.

I put down the letter and looked out of the window again. In a moment the bell would go for afternoon classes. I found myself remembering the first time I had seen Bryan. He was the quarry and I was the hunter then. It had been exciting. But once we'd had that wonderful dinner together, I'd begun to think of him as a friend. In those strange nine days at Treetops I'd lurched from one role to another. What was I, friend or foe? Confidante or stranger-spy? Right up till that fateful moment when I'd placed the Saint Christopher medal on the table and committed myself. And brought on myself the pain of his rejection. *Oh, well, I guess it's all part of growing up,* I told myself. *Serves me right for letting myself get involved.*

I sighed, and folded the letter and left it on my desk next to my French homework, promising myself that I'd write back to Amanda that evening. The bell rang and I pushed the memory of Bryan out of my head and went downstairs.

The next letter greeted me in mid October, when I got back to school after the Thanksgiving weekend.

Hi, Sandra. Hope you had a great holiday. Bry and I went to Treetops for a Thanksgiving celebration with Mom and Dad and Gran. I told them I was writing to you and they send their best wishes. It really was a celebration and Mom cooked up a storm. Remember that last dinner? Such a super spread, but then I brought the bell in on a cushion, and Bry was so pleased, waiting for Dad's reaction. And it all fell apart. Disaster.

Poor Bry! He minded much more than I did. It was all his plan, you see, something he could do for Dad. I suddenly thought that it was like your plan to find out what really happened to Christopher, something you could do for your mom. After I'd had this Brilliant Insight (neat, eh? We're studying insights and foreshadowings in Eng. Lit. this year), I told Bry about it. I thought he'd shrug it off, but he didn't. He actually listened. Then I didn't say anything more. Now that I'm practically in my teens I'm working on Tact, which Gran tells me is something I desperately need, though I must say I've never thought about it before. Anyway, I hope I'm not being really tactless now, but don't be too surprised if you get a letter from Bry before long.

Lots of love, Amanda.

I won't hold my breath, I promised myself as I tucked the letter back in its envelope; but in spite of my resolve, I found myself watching the mail. I was more than a little disappointed when October gave way to November without a letter, and then it was the Christmas holidays and I had *still* not heard from Bryan. *Forget it,* I told myself. *That chapter's closed.*

By springtime I *had* forgotten, and when a letter arrived at school with a Toronto postmark and unfamiliar handwriting on the envelope, I puzzled over it before finally tearing it open.

Dear Sandra, You'll probably be surprised to hear from me after all this time. Please go on reading. Don't get mad and tear this letter up—though I wouldn't blame you—

As if I would! My heart thumped uncomfortably and I told myself not to be stupid. It was a bit late for an apology, but I figured that's what the letter would be. A formal apology. Amanda had probably forgotten her "tact" and had been nagging him.

. . . because this isn't a formal apology, though I certainly owe you a big one. It's more than that. It's an invitation for you to come and stay at Treetops this summer, as soon as school's out, if that's okay with you and your family. I know we can't go back to where we were before—but that wasn't a real relationship anyway, was it? We each had our own agenda. What I'm hoping is that you'll agree to a new beginning so that we can become genuine friends. Please come. There's a piece of unfinished business I'd like you to be part of . . .

New beginnings? I thought. *Are they really possible?* Could Bryan and I leave all the old stuff behind? It would be a bit like immigrating to a new country. Finding new ways, a new language, new friends. People did that all the time. So maybe learning to be friends again wouldn't be too difficult.

"No, I won't have you meet me with the boat," I replied to his next more detailed letter. "Mom and Dad say I may borrow the car. I should be at Treetops in time for lunch on the 14th . . ."

And then we'll see whether I stay, or whether it's all a dreadful mistake, I told myself as I addressed the envelope.

So here I was once more, on familiar ground, cautiously negotiating my way down the steep driveway from the highway and pulling up on the forecourt in front of the house. I had barely taken the key from the ignition when the door was flung open and Amanda ran out.

A year had changed her. She was taller, with the beginnings of a figure, and she'd let her red-blond hair grow. But she was as full of pep as ever. *No comparisons,* I warned myself as I got out of the car. *No looking back.* But then I was swept into a bear hug and found myself hugging her back as though nothing had changed.

Then Bryan came out of the house, and it was really weird. I couldn't move or say anything. I just stood frozen beside the car, my arm still around Amanda.

"Hi," he said.

"Thanks for inviting me," I managed to reply.

"Oh, you two!" Amanda groaned. "You're hopeless. Don't just stand there, Bry. Take in Sandra's luggage. Is this case all there is? You've got the guest room this time—no Uncle Greg, ha ha! He doesn't show his face around here any more, thank goodness."

"I suppose not." I remembered his facetious remarks about Cassandra, the prophet of ill omen.

"Mom says that what happened last summer was actually the best thing for him—you see, he couldn't sponge on Dad any more. Either he was going to starve or he'd have to get his act together, so that's what he's done. He's working for some ad agency and doing quite well, Mom says. So you don't have to feel sorry for him. Mom's in the kitchen. Oh, I should warn you. Since she and Dad went to Asia she's got into Thai cooking—interesting, I guess you could say. I hope you don't mind it."

"I love it." I laughed and followed Amanda into the kitchen, to be swept by Margaret into a hug scented with lemon grass and lime.

"Thank you for coming, my dear. We're so glad you didn't refuse—which you might well have done, all things considered."

"Please don't think of it, Margaret," I said quickly. "The past's over and done with."

Bryan came upstairs. "I've put your case in the guest room."

"Thanks."

"You're welcome."

Amanda threw up her hands dramatically. "If that's the best you two can do, I give up. Is lunch ready, Mom?"

"Five minutes. I think it's warm enough to eat on the deck, don't you? You can take the plates and cutlery outside."

So in many ways the meal was like my first one at Treetops the year before. It was a pleasant lunch, but full of memories I couldn't quite discount.

Don and Margaret talked enthusiastically about their holiday, and I managed to ask the right sort of questions about Thailand, but I was thankful when Amanda jumped to her feet.

"Please, may Bryan and Sandra and I be excused? We've got things to do."

As I followed them down the steps towards the dock, I felt as if I were reliving the previous summer. Then I suddenly stopped. Surely they weren't planning another diving expedition? Not to *Far Skimmer*?

"It's all right, Sandra," Amanda urged. "It's just a small ceremony. We thought of it last winter, but we decided to save it till you were here. We wanted you to be part of it."

We reached the dock and Bryan dropped the sports bag he was carrying into the runabout. There was no diving gear. No tanks. He turned to help me aboard and then sat in the stern and started the engine while Amanda cast off. A mix of memories, happy, sad and horrible, flooded over me. I sat silently, my hands laced around my knees, while Bryan steered away from shore and between the small islands out towards the site of the wreck.

I recognized the familiar markers with a growing feeling of dread: the radio tower and the jack pine, the fixed light on the island and the buoy. I turned on Bryan and Amanda with anger. "Why'd you bring me back here? Bryan, you talked about new beginnings in your letter. I thought you meant it. Coming out here is horrible. How could you be so cruel?"

143

"Hold on, Sandra. It's just one last piece of unfinished business. Amanda and I both want you to be a witness to it. Please trust me." He cut the engine and we drifted silently on the sun-dazzled water.

Then he went on. "We've decided that we'll never explore *Far Skimmer*. She's off-limits. I'm glad they didn't have to try to raise her for the inquest. She's kind of like a memorial to your uncle. That's one thing. And the other is that Dad never wanted the bell—I certainly got that one wrong. So we're going to return it to where it belongs."

He unzipped the sports bag and lifted it out. It gleamed golden in the sun. He ran his fingers over the inscription. *"Far Skimmer,"* he said aloud. "This is where it all began. The bell called to Dad so that he could never forget what he'd done. It called to me so that I would try to stop its tolling, though I didn't know what it was tolling for—only Dad and Uncle Greg knew that. And it called to you, Sandra, and brought you into our lives. What you found out was so horrible, I couldn't bear it. But Amanda's helped me to understand that it really brought us the truth—"

"To make us all free," Amanda chimed in.

"Yes. So now the time's come to return the bell to its proper home. Its job is done."

"Don't forget the next bit," Amanda prompted.

"I won't." Bryan held the bell aloft with one hand and rang the clapper. One, two. Three, four. Five, six. Seven, eight. "We didn't know whether sailors rang the ship's bell a special number of times for a burial at sea, or whether they even rang it at all. But Amanda and I decided to ring it eight times—for his age. In remembrance of Christopher Steven Henderson."

144

He held the bell over the side of the boat and let it fall into the water. For a second it gleamed just beneath the surface, but then it tipped, the air spilled out and it was gone.

I blinked back unexpected tears. "Thank you both. That was beautiful."

"Back we go then, Bry," Amanda ordered. "Now we can begin all over again."

I watched Bryan as he started the engine. He looked up and caught my glance. He smiled, his blue eyes once more warm and friendly, and I was able to smile back. *Begin all over again,* Amanda had said.

Do you know, I told myself, suddenly happy enough to want to dance—only a small runabout was no place for dancing—*I think it's going to be all right!*